The Body in the Basement

NORAH McCLINTOCK

The Body in the Basement

cover by
Wesley Lowe

Scholastic Canada Ltd.

Toronto, New York, London, Sydney, Auckland

Scholastic Canada Ltd.
123 Newkirk Road, Richmond Hill, Ontario, Canada L4C 3G5

Scholastic Inc.
555 Broadway, New York, NY 10012, USA

Scholastic Australia Pty Limited
PO Box 579, Gosford, NSW 2250, Australia

Scholastic New Zealand Ltd.
Private Bag 94407, Greenmount, Auckland, New Zealand

Scholastic Ltd.
Villiers House, Clarendon Avenue, Leamington Spa,
Warwickshire CV32 5PR, UK

Canadian Cataloguing in Publication Data

McClintock, Norah
  The body in the basement

ISBN 0-590-24983-5

I. Title.

PS8575.C62B62 1997   jC813'.54   C96-932596-7
PZ7.M33Bo 1997

Other books by Norah McClintock:

Shakespeare and Legs
The Stepfather Game
Jack's Back
Mistaken Identity

Chapter One

If she lived to be a hundred and two, and forgot everything about herself — her name, the date she was born, the house she grew up in — Tasha Scanlan knew that she would always remember the morning when it all started.

Jace Bhupal was leaning against the door to the computer lab, giving her a running commentary as he flipped through the morning paper. She was pawing frantically through the notebooks and loose-leaf binders on the top shelf of her locker, searching for her Chemistry homework.

"They call it urban renewal," Jace muttered in disgust. "What they should call it is bulldozing history. Just look at this." He thrust the paper under Tasha's nose.

"Not now," Tasha said. She liked Jace a lot. More than a lot, in fact. They were best friends. But he had a tendency to go on — and on — about things like computers, or electronic gadgets, or, as he was

1

doing now, buildings of historic significance. "If I don't hand in my assignment, Sparling's going to take ten points off my mid-term grade."

"But they're tearing down one of this city's landmarks," Jace said, "a place that opened its doors back in the 1920s and operated right up until a year ago. Name me one other restaurant in this city with that kind of staying power. You can't, can you? That's because there's not many places that can compare with the old Fireside Café."

Tasha stiffened. "Did you say, Fireside Café?"

"Yeah. Why? You know it?"

Tasha shook her head, as if to clear it. Oh, yes, she knew the Fireside Café. But it, like her mother, was best forgotten. Dwelling on the past couldn't bring it back. She'd become expert at shoving memories of her mother and the Café out of her mind, as if she were going through a closet and throwing out old clothes that no longer fit. If her mother wanted nothing to do with Tasha, then Tasha wanted nothing to do with her . . . at least, that's what she told herself.

Then curiosity got the better of her. She dropped her Biology notes, straightened up, and snatched the paper out of Jace's hands. A photo on page three showed a dilapidated version of a place she remembered vividly. Although it looked run down, it was the same Fireside Café that had been owned by her family for decades. And now they were tearing it down? Tasha wondered if her father knew, and if he did, why he hadn't said anything to her.

Jace was frowning at her. "Tasha, you okay?"

She nodded, but she felt far from okay. Her head

spun. Her stomach churned. "The Fireside Café used to belong to my great-grandfather," she said. "He opened it a year before the big stock market crash in 1929 and ran it right through the Depression in the 1930s. After the Second World War, my grandfather ran it. Then my parents took over from him."

Jace whistled softly. He looked impressed. "How come you never told me?"

She shrugged. "My father sold the place before I met you — about five years ago."

"Well, whoever he sold it to obviously didn't run it well. The wrecking ball is scheduled to swing at nine a.m. — " He checked his watch. "In exactly ten minutes. And that'll be the end of that."

Tasha stared at the photo in the paper, feeling as if she were looking back into a previous life. From the name over the big picture window to the heavy grey stone of the exterior, everything looked exactly as she remembered it. Well, almost exactly. The little flower boxes that used to run the length of the huge front window were empty. For as long as Tasha could remember, they had held tulips in early spring and geraniums in summer. The gabled windows on the second floor, the ones that had been covered with snowy-white lace curtains, gaped like blind eyes. Weeds were growing up through the cracks of the flagstone patio where once, in summer, tables had been set up so customers could eat al fresco.

"I practically grew up there," Tasha said. "We used to live just a couple of blocks away. When I was small, my dad was the Café's chef, and my mother managed the place. That was before my father started his own restaurant."

Jace nodded. Like almost everyone Tasha knew, he was familiar with the Lenny and Denny's restaurant chain.

"My mother went back to school when I was little, so they hired someone else to manage the place. But they still owned it." She stared again at the picture in the paper, and her mind flooded with more memories — the crackle of the fire that her father used to light in the big stone fireplace every night from November to the end of March, the fragrant blending of wood burning and turkey or beef or lamb roasting in the ovens in the kitchen, the tinkle of silverware, the hushed buzz of conversation. And, best of all, the scent of her mother's perfume, the silky smoothness of her arms as she wrapped them around Tasha to hug her, the glow of her mother's face as she threw back her head to laugh. How her mother had loved to laugh . . .

"You want me to drive you over there at lunch?" Jace asked. "Maybe we can find you a souvenir, something from the place that you can take home."

Tasha shook her head. The Fireside Café, like her mother, was best forgotten. Already, thoughts of her mother were making her stomach churn, and the old sadness well up again. "Thanks," she said, "but I don't think so."

"You sure?"

"Absolutely sure," Tasha said. She pushed all thought of the Fireside Café from her mind and resumed the search for her Chemistry homework.

She didn't say a word about the Café for the rest

4

of the day, or even mention it that night when her father came home from work. Easier just to let the bitter memories fade away. The subject might never have come up if Denny Durant, her father's partner in Lenny and Denny's, hadn't barged in just as she and her father were sitting down to supper.

"I can't believe this is happening," Denny boomed, striding past Tasha without even saying hello. "I can't believe you're *letting* it happen, Len. And nobody *told* me. Nobody said a word." The louder his voice got — and it got louder with every word — the redder his face became.

Leonard Scanlan looked up from his lemon chicken and smiled.

Tasha could never understand why he always seemed amused by Denny's excitable, grating personality. But then, she'd never been able to fathom how the two had remained partners for as long as they had. Denny was a big, burly, battered looking man who'd been a rough but popular pro hockey player before retiring into the restaurant business. Her father was his exact opposite, a slim, serious, somewhat moody man who knew nothing about sports but everything about cooking. Denny's loud voice and demanding tone never bothered Leonard Scanlan, but they sure got on Tasha's nerves. She sat down, still without a hello from him, and started to eat her meal.

"I assume you're talking about the Fireside Café," Tasha's father said.

"You bet I am. Is it asking too much for one guy to pick up the phone and tell another guy what's going on?"

"You've been out of the country for six weeks, Denny," Leonard Scanlan said reasonably. "You didn't call even once from your vacation to check on the business, even though you knew we were going through an audit. I had enough to do handling my job, plus yours, plus answering all the accountants' questions. Under the circumstances, you can hardly expect to be kept up to date with every minor event in the city."

"*Minor* event?" Denny exploded. "Tearing down the Fireside Café is a minor event to you?" His eyes narrowed. "Did you know about this, Lenny?"

Leonard Scanlan shrugged. "I knew Jerry Malone had died, but I never thought this was going to happen."

"Who's Jerry Malone?" Tasha asked.

"The last owner of the Café," her father replied. "He died a couple of weeks ago. I went to the funeral. His son didn't say anything about selling the place, let alone tearing it down. He must have had it planned, though. You can't get a sale through and a building torn down that fast. Maybe he set it all rolling while Jerry was still in the hospital."

"Little weasel," Denny muttered. "I always told you you should have kept that place, Lenny. But no, you were the one in charge. We could have turned it into a new Lenny and Denny's."

"*We* couldn't have afforded to buy it," Leonard Scanlan snapped. "Look, Denny, about that audit — about our finances in general — we have to talk. Tomorrow, okay? I want you in the office first thing in the morning."

"I can't believe that little weasel tore the place down. I can't believe Jerry left the place to such an ungrateful little creep. Didn't he know how much history the place had, how much tradition?"

"Did you hear what I said, Denny?"

"But the Café —"

"Denny!" Impatience flickered in Leonard Scanlan's eyes. Tasha felt her stomach constricting. Whenever that look came onto her father's face, it meant trouble. In a moment, if Denny didn't drop the subject of the Café and focus instead on the audit, whatever that was about, her father would hit the roof. Ever since she had been a little girl, the sound of his shouting had upset her.

"Forget the Café. It's too late," Leonard Scanlan said, his voice tight. "Besides, if anyone should be upset about the Fireside Café being torn down, it's me, Denny, not you."

Denny seemed to sense that he had crossed some dangerous line, and threw up his hands in surrender. "Okay, okay," he said. "Consider the subject closed, unless, of course, you ever decide you want to re-open it."

"I won't," Leonard Scanlan said, and smiled. Relief washed over Tasha. "Are you sure you're not hungry?"

"Yeah, I'm sure," Denny grumbled as he got up to leave.

"Tomorrow morning, Den," Leonard called after him. "First thing. We have to talk."

"Yeah, yeah."

After Denny left, Tasha waited to see if her father would say anything else about the Fireside

Café. She was glad when he didn't. She'd been afraid that news of the demolition would stir up the bitter memories and make him sad all over again. But when he finished his supper he made himself a cup of espresso and settled down in front of the television to watch a documentary on white lions.

Tasha thought that was that as far as the Fireside Café was concerned.

She was mistaken.

* * *

The next evening, while reaching for a cleaver to chop up some beef for stew, Leonard Scanlan flipped on the little television on the kitchen counter so he could watch the news while he worked. A still shot of the Café flashed onto the screen, followed by footage of a wrecking ball smashing into its stone exterior, crumpling it as if it were cardboard.

Tasha glanced at the screen as she diced raw potatoes. Standing against a backdrop of the demolished Café, a reporter stared into the camera. "Who would have guessed that a terrible secret lay hidden in the basement of one of this city's landmark restaurants?" he was saying. "Workers today discovered a body buried beneath the old Fireside Café, which was demolished only yesterday. Police are so far refusing to comment on how long the unidentified body may have lain in its concrete grave, nor have they offered any theory as to the cause of death."

Tasha stared at her father, whose eyes didn't waver from the screen. "Dad?" she said. "Daddy?"

Leonard Scanlan shook his head slowly as he tore his gaze away from the television. "You never know, do you?" he murmured softly. "Buildings can be just like people. You're pretty sure you know everything there is to know about them, and then you dig a little deeper and, surprise, you get a nasty shock."

Tasha glanced back at the television, but too late. Instead of the dust kicked up around the ruins of the Café, she saw a chorus line of dancing tubes of toothpaste. When she wondered aloud about the body that had been found in the basement of the Café, her father chided her for being ghoulish.

"I don't have the same morbid curiosity that seems to afflict so many people these days," he said. "If you don't mind, I'd rather leave all the speculation to the police."

"But, Dad, a body in the basement — "

"I mean it, Tasha."

That night, Tasha couldn't sleep. That body must have lain beneath the Café since the 1920s, maybe even earlier. She'd read about how wild things had been in some places after the First World War. They'd called that decade the Roaring Twenties, and it had been an age of extremes — jazz, prohibition, rum-running gangsters. For all she knew the Café might have been a nightclub before her family bought it. Maybe some notorious gangster had been murdered there. She wondered what her great-grandfather would have thought if he'd discovered that the foundations of his restaurant hid such a grisly secret. But that wasn't the only thing that kept going through her mind.

Hearing so much about the Café again made her think of her mother, something she tried never to do. Every time she closed her eyes, there was the laughing face of Catherine Scanlan. There, too, were the shouts and accusations, the angry banging, the slamming of doors the night her mother left. Tasha had cried that night. She'd cried for days afterward, while her father rocked her and told her, over and over, "She'll be back, honey. One of these days, she'll be back." But she never was, except in Tasha's dreams.

Chapter Two

The next morning, over a cup of coffee that did little to banish the woolly-headed feeling of a sleepless night, Tasha scoured the newspaper for more news about the Fireside Café. There was none. Not a word.

"Are you *sure* you're okay?" Jace said, glancing over at her for the tenth time in less than two blocks.

"I'm fine," Tasha said. "But I won't be for long if you don't keep your eyes on the road."

"I'm worried about you," Jace said. "No offense, but you look like sh— "

"You always come up with the absolute perfect thing to say," Tasha said.

"I just meant — "

"I know what you meant. That I look like — "

"You look terrific," Jace said.

"That's *not* what you said."

Jace shrugged. "You looked *really* tired. Other than that, though, you look terrific."

Tasha smirked. "Smooth," she said. "Very smooth." She ran a hand through her thick brown hair. "Seriously, I'm fine. I've just been thinking about the Café. It's brought back a lot of memories."

Jace nodded.

They drove the rest of the way to school in comfortable silence. This was something Tasha liked about Jace. She could spend hours with him, studying or watching a movie or just hanging out in the park, without feeling that they always had to be talking. They had met four years ago, shortly after Tasha and her father moved into the neighbourhood where Jace lived, and even though he was a year older than her they'd become fast friends. There was nothing she and Jace couldn't talk about. Well, almost nothing.

Lately, Tasha had been wondering about the nature of their friendship. She'd found herself imagining what it would be like to stroll down the street holding Jace's hand, or to wander along the boardwalk with his arm around her shoulder or her waist. She'd taken to glancing furtively at him, drawn by his sparkling brown eyes, wondering exactly when they had changed, at what moment they had become so mesmerizing, and why it had taken her so long to notice. Or contemplating his mouth, which was usually smiling, and imagining how it might feel if he were to press his lips to hers. She'd think these things and then she'd think: Idiot, we're just friends. Friends don't daydream about each other. But lately, too, when she'd spotted other girls, girls in Jace's year, looking at him in the same way she did, she felt uneasy. She wondered whether he had invited any of them to the spring dance, or whether any of them had invited him. She wondered, but didn't ask, because it was one question she lacked the courage to pose. She didn't think she'd be able to stand it if she didn't get the answer she wanted.

When they got to school, Jace glanced at his watch and said, "I'll catch up with you at lunch, okay?"

"You in a hurry to be somewhere?" Tasha asked.

He shrugged and looked away from her. "I have to meet someone. I have this new program I promised to share." He patted his jacket pocket where, Tasha knew, he always carried two or three floppy disks, usually containing some weird new program he'd been working on.

"See you at lunch, then," she said.

He nodded and scurried away across the parking lot. Tasha walked more slowly into the school, and found Rick Jansen in front of her locker. He stood aside, smiling at her, while she opened her locker door and found the books she needed for History and Biology. She smiled back, and wondered what he wanted. Rick was in three of her classes, and had been staring at her a lot lately. There were plenty of times, like now, when she was sure he wanted to say something to her, but every time she glanced at him, he grinned awkwardly and looked away. It was unnerving. Now here he was, looking down at the toes of his very large feet like some big bashful kid.

Tasha decided to put the poor guy out of his misery. "You ready for the French quiz this morning?" she asked.

He grinned at her. "I guess I'm as ready as I'll ever be," he said. "How about you?"

Tasha nodded. The pause that followed made Rick squirm. Tasha groped for something, anything, to say to end his torture. "I hope he doesn't give us one of those long translations to do. Remember that last one? That was the hardest French paragraph I've ever struggled through."

"Me, too," Rick said. Then the bell rang. Tasha couldn't remember when she'd been happier to hear it. As she hurried to her first class, she caught a glimpse of Jace down the hall. She raised a hand and started to call to him, but her voice died in her throat when she saw him lean forward and kiss the girl he was with. She was so stunned she stopped where she stood. Someone behind her slammed into her. Tasha heard but paid no attention to the muttering of the boy who now squeezed around her. Jace had kissed Sharon Wong, a girl who was in his grade and, from what Tasha knew, in most of his classes. She felt like she'd been kicked in the stomach.

For the next few days she avoided Jace. She wasn't sure if it was to keep him from telling her about some date he had with Sharon Wong, or if she just didn't trust herself to be friendly to him when she felt so disappointed. After all, he was her friend, not her boyfriend. He could date whoever he wanted, right? But despite how logical she tried to be, she still felt let down, almost betrayed.

She was sitting in English class on Friday afternoon, listening to Ms Cardoso read a Shakespearean sonnet, when she happened to glance over at the door. She wasn't sure why she looked away from the teacher. She'd been enjoying the lyrical words of the poem and the melodic lilt of Ms Cardoso's voice — they were almost making her forget about Jace. She wasn't bored like the kids who congregated at the back of the class. But she looked up — and was stunned to find her father standing at the classroom door. His presence was so unexpected, so unlikely, that for a moment she thought she was seeing things. But no, he was really there, and even though the door was open, he knocked on it. Ms Cardoso stopped reading. She crossed the front of the room and exchanged hushed words with Tasha's father. Then she turned and beckoned to Tasha.

Tasha knew, as she walked up the aisle toward the door, that something was wrong. Her father had never appeared at her school in the middle of the day before. She'd rarely seen such a sombre expression on his face. He laid a hand on her shoulder and guided her down the hall, away from the classroom. He didn't say a word.

"Dad, what's wrong?"

Her father peered into her eyes for what seemed an eternity. His face was almost grey. His shoulders slumped, like a man weary to the point of collapse. "I wanted you to hear it from me first," he said. "I didn't want someone else to tell you, or for you to hear it on the radio or TV."

Now she was convinced something was terribly wrong. "Hear what, Dad?" she managed. Her voice echoed in her ears. Was she really shouting, or were her ears playing tricks on her? "What's happened?"

"It's your mother," he said. "She . . . she's been found."

Her mother, found! A jumble of memories flooded Tasha's mind — glossy chestnut hair, sleek tanned arms, a crisp chef's apron, merry laughter — and her heart soared. But why did her father look so terrible, like he'd aged a few decades since breakfast? She waited for him to continue, breathing in and out slowly and carefully, willing herself to stay calm, but her mind was churning. To be *found*, someone first had to be lost. But her mother wasn't lost. She was just absent. *Voluntarily* absent. No, this couldn't be good news.

"Tasha, she's . . . " Her father's voice broke off. He started to sob, and swiped at his tears with the back of his hand. "Oh, Tasha, she's dead."

At that moment Tasha crossed over into a nightmare world. Every emotion was heightened. Time slowed to a crawl. The impossible seemed frighteningly real.

This can't be happening, she thought, standing in the grim silence of the school's second floor hallway . My mother is *gone*, she left us five years ago. But *dead*? She can't be.

She stared at her father, who had found a tissue in one of his jacket pockets and was wiping at his eyes. "But . . . but how?" she asked. "What happened? Was she — Daddy? — " She gripped his arm, " — was she in some kind of accident?"

Her father shook his head. His face was twisted in such agony that Tasha felt herself tremble. The answer, she feared, would be even more horrible than the news she'd already received.

"We should go home," he said in a strangely hushed voice.

"But, Dad . . ."

"I'll tell you everything, Tasha. But not here."
He glanced down the hallway. Tasha followed his
gaze. The clock above the water fountain. The long
hallway. In a couple of minutes the bell would ring
and the hall would be flooded with kids and teach-
ers, and they'd all stare at her father, who, although
he seemed to be trying to stop, was still crying.

"Okay, Dad," she whispered. She followed him
down the stairs and out of the school. Each step
seemed to be one more step away from hope, away
from a belief that she'd clung to all these years —
that a change of heart or a moment of longing would
bring her mother home again. That would never
happen now. It was too late.

The trip home took only a few silent minutes.
Tasha's father seemed to be focussing all his attention on his driving, and Tasha let him. She couldn't
trust herself to speak, anyway. There would be time
for the details when they got home.

* * *

A grey car sat at the curb directly outside the Scanlan house. Two people, a man and a woman, got out
of it as Tasha's father steered his car into the driveway. By the time he took the key out of the ignition,
the two strangers were standing beside the car,
waiting.

Tasha looked anxiously at her father. "Who are
they?" she asked.

"Police officers, I expect," Tasha's father said.
"Let's pray it's not the press."

Police officers? "What do they want?"

"I guess we'll find out." Leonard Scanlan

sighed. He drew in a deep breath, as if to steel himself for the encounter, then got out of the car. Tasha saw the glint of a badge in the sunlight. They *were* police officers.

"We'd like to ask you a few questions, Mr. Scanlan," the man said. He smiled at Tasha as she got out of the car, but it didn't seem like a friendly smile.

"This is my daughter Tasha," her father said, then added, as if to explain, "Natasha."

The man nodded. "I'm Detective Pirelli. This is Detective Marchand."

Tasha nodded. She'd never met a police detective before, and wondered what these two wanted.

They all trooped into the house. Tasha's father hesitated, offered tea or coffee, seemed at a loss as to what to do.

"We need to ask you some questions about your wife, sir, " Detective Pirelli said.

Leonard Scanlan looked at the two detectives, then at Tasha.

"I — I haven't told my daughter," he said, his voice almost breaking under the strain of the five simple words. "If I could just have a moment . . . "

The detectives exchanged glances. "How old are you, Tasha?" Detective Marchand asked.

"Fifteen," Tasha whispered. Why did they want to know that? What did her age have to do with anything?

The detective nodded as if satisfied. "Take as much time as you need," she said to Tasha's father. "We'll wait in here." She and Detective Pirelli went into the living room. Tasha's father laid a hand on her shoulder and steered her toward the kitchen.

"What's going on, Dad?" Tasha demanded. "Why are *they* here?" She couldn't make sense of any of it. Her mother was dead, and now there were two police officers in the living room, waiting to talk to her father. Something very bad was going on.

"It's about what they found buried . . . buried under the Café," he began. He wasn't even looking at her. He was staring out the kitchen window.

"What?" Tasha asked. Why didn't he just come out and tell her what was happening? Then, like a car crash, it hit her. "Mom?" she said, her voice choked with the horror of the image that floated before her eyes. "You don't mean that Mom . . . " No, it couldn't be. "That it was Mom buried . . . " She couldn't say it. Nothing could make her say it.

When her father finally turned to face her, his cheeks were wet with tears.

"It's not true," Tasha cried. "It's not her." Shouting now. "It's not true!"

"Tasha, please . . . "

All of a sudden Detective Marchand was in the kitchen, standing beside Tasha's father, talking to Tasha, her large blue eyes filled with concern. "Your mother was buried for a long time," she said in a voice so soft and soothing that Tasha wondered whether she ever had trouble getting criminals to take her seriously. "We think about five years."

No. No! "It's not her," Tasha said. "It's not my mother." This couldn't be happening. This was something that belonged in a movie — a horror movie — not something that was part of her life.

"When we have a case like this, Tasha, there are

procedures we follow to make an identification. Whenever we can we use dental records. They can be really helpful in telling us what we need to know. Sometimes we get lucky and find other things that can help us. Like a piece of jewellery."

Tasha held her breath while Detective Marchand burrowed in her jacket pocket. She pulled out a small plastic bag, and held it flat on her hand for Tasha to see. Inside the bag was a diamond ring. Tasha's fingers trembled as she reached for it. She peered inside the silver band for the words she knew were etched there, but tears blinded her.

"Tasha, honey . . . "

She felt her father's arm around her shoulders, and collapsed against it, crying. "When you said she was dead, I thought — " Tasha began, sobbing. It took a few moments before she could speak again. Detective Marchand thrust a small wad of tissues into her hand. "I thought maybe she'd had an accident. I thought maybe she'd been hit by a car or something. But this . . . " She sobbed into the tissues.

"It's really important that we talk to your father now," Detective Marchand said after a few more moments.

"Please, Tasha, go up to your room," Leonard Scanlan said.

"But I want to know what happened. This is about Mom. I have a right to know."

"Tasha, please." Her father's eyes, his quivering voice, his crumpled face all pleaded with her.

"Will you tell me everything they say?" She didn't care that Detective Marchand was still in the room.

He nodded.

"*Everything*, Dad. Promise?"

"I promise."

She kissed his damp cheek and walked out of the kitchen while he and Detective Marchand went into the living room. She went a third of the way up the stairs. Then, out of sight, she crouched down to listen to what they were saying. She had a right to know.

"Can you tell us about the last time you saw your wife, Mr. Scanlan." That was Detective Pirelli's voice.

Tasha heard her father's voice deep in his chest as he spoke. "It was five years ago," he said. "The night of August second."

A pause before Detective Pirelli spoke again. He sounded suspicious. "You remember the exact date?"

"It was the night of the big storm," Leonard Scanlan replied. "The night Hurricane Bradley did all that damage."

Tasha remembered it as if it were only a few days ago, instead of years. The night had been slick and black. The wind had howled like a wild animal all night. And Tasha had cowered in her bed, terrified by the wailing outside her window that somehow did not drown out the terrible shouting in the kitchen, directly below her bedroom.

"Can you tell us what happened that night, sir?" Detective Pirelli prompted.

"My wife and I had an argument . . . "

Their shouting had awakened Tasha. At first she'd pulled the covers up over her head to try to block out the angry bark of their voices. She couldn't remember exactly when they'd started arguing. It seemed at the time that they were always at odds. They even fought in public — in a mall, on the street outside their house, in the Café. Tasha hated when they did that. People turned to stare at them. Once when they'd argued in the restaurant, Tasha's father had been so angry that he'd shouted, "One of these days, Catherine, you're going to push me too far."

"What were you arguing about?" Detective Pirelli asked.

"Me," Tasha whispered to herself. They were arguing about me . . . *"I'm thirty-five years old, Leonard," her mother had shouted. "If I can't do what I want now, when can I?" "But you have a child," her father had said. "I want a life, Leonard. A life!" Up in her room, ten-year-old Tasha heard those words and knew instantly that all the shouting and anger were her fault. Her parents were fighting because of her. She had wrapped her arms around her knees and rocked herself and wished that she had slept through the storm outside, and the one raging in her kitchen . . .*

"Mr. Scanlan," Detective Pirelli was saying, "can you remember what you and your wife were arguing about?"

It took a few moments before Leonard Scanlan answered. "We argued about everything," he said. "We weren't getting along very well. I guess that night was the last straw."

"What do you mean, sir, the last straw?"

"We had the biggest blow-up of our marriage,

and Catherine left. She walked out on me."

Tasha remembered that the shouting had stopped very suddenly. She'd been crouching on the floor in the corner of her room, beside the vent to the kitchen, listening. She waited, but heard only footsteps. Abruptly, the front door slammed.

"Did she say where she was going?"

"No."

"What happened after she left?"

"Nothing," Tasha's father said. "I was angry and tired. Eventually I went to bed. I never saw her again."

"She made no contact with you after that?"

"She wrote a few times. I received a couple of letters from Vancouver."

Tasha remembered those letters. She had practically memorized them as she read them over and over, searching for some clue that her mother had forgiven her for being a burden, and would one day return. The letters had been agonizingly brief: *Have settled into a nice rooming house. Am making plans for departure.* Neutral words, short sentences, conveying nothing. But always a few words for Tasha. *Kisses to my Tasha–Taters*, one said, using Tasha's childhood nickname, an echo of her passion for potatoes — mashed, fried, boiled, baked, it didn't matter. *Hugs for Tasha–Taters.* Beyond that, nothing. Tasha could find no clue that might hint at her mother's return.

"So after she left here, she went to Vancouver," Detective Pirelli said. "Do you have any idea how long she was there?"

"I really can't say. As I said, she wrote a couple

of times. After that, we never heard from her again."

"Nothing at all?"

No answer. Tasha imagined her father shaking his head.

"Did you make an attempt to locate your wife after that, Mr. Scanlan?"

"My wife left *me*," he snapped, his voice prickly, the way she remembered it whenever the subject of Tasha's mother came up. Over the years, that tone had made Tasha afraid to ask her father anything about her mother. "She made it quite clear that she wanted nothing to do with me, with Tasha, or with the restaurant. She'd been planning to go for months. She'd even sold me her half of the Café so she'd have money to live on. If she hadn't left that night, she would have gone a week later, maybe a month later."

"Your wife walked out on you, and except for a few letters never contacted you or your daughter again, and you didn't find that unusual? You didn't try to contact her?"

"She was the one who wanted out," Leonard Scanlan said. "Not me. I thought she'd contact *me* if and when she was ever interested."

"Do you still have the letters your wife wrote?" Detective Marchand asked.

"No, I don't."

Tasha stiffened. Her father had taken those letters from her for safekeeping. He'd said she'd wear them out if she kept folding and unfolding them.

"I had them for a while." Her father again. "Then I tore them up and threw them out. No point living in the past."

Tasha couldn't believe what she was hearing. Those letters had been all she had of her mother. He'd promised to take care of them, and he'd broken his promise.

"Do you remember if they had a return address on them?" Detective Pirelli said.

"They didn't," Tasha murmured, her voice echoing her father's reply. She knew, because she'd wanted so desperately to write to her mother, to beg her to come home.

"Do you remember when you received the last letter?"

"I guess it was about six or seven months after she walked out on me."

There was silence for a moment, then Detective Marchand said, "Do you know anyone who might have had a reason to kill your wife?"

"I most certainly do not," Tasha's father said.

"And you have no idea how she ended up at the Fireside Café when she was supposed to have been in Vancouver?"

"I do not."

"She never contacted you, other than by letter, after she left?"

"Never."

"And you yourself were home here that whole night?"

A pause. "My daughter was ten years old at the time, officer. I couldn't leave her alone. In fact, as I recall, I had to go upstairs and comfort her after her mother left."

Tasha wrapped her arms around her knees and held herself close. Her father was a good man, a hard-working man. He had taken good care of her ever since her mother had left. He had taught her to be truthful, to always do the right thing, no matter how difficult that might be. It was only because she didn't want the police to get the wrong idea about him that she made herself sit exactly where she was, that she stopped herself from going down and contradicting him.

Chapter Three

When Tasha heard the two detectives get up to leave, she crept up the stairs out of sight. But she couldn't make herself stay there, not when there was so much she still needed to know. She ran back downstairs. "How did it happen?" she asked the two detectives. They looked blankly at her, as if they didn't understand. "How was my mother . . . " Here she stumbled. "How did she — " the word was so difficult " — die?"

Her father's face drained of colour. "Please, Tasha, don't," he begged.

"Sometimes it's better not to know everything," Detective Marchand said.

Tasha drew herself up straight so that she looked as adult as everyone else in the front hall, and as determined to know the truth as they were to keep it from her. "For the last five years, I thought my mother was living happily on the other side of the country," she said. "I even started to hate her for it. I thought she'd forgotten all about me, or that she didn't care. But I never stopped hoping she'd come back. I prayed for a letter or a phone call. Anything. Now I find out that all this time she — " It was so hard. She didn't think that it would ever become easier. "I think I have a right to know how it happened."

Detective Marchand came so close that Tasha saw purple flecks in her deep blue eyes. They were the prettiest eyes she'd ever seen. "I'll tell you if you really want to know," Detective Marchand said, her voice as soft as silk. "But first I want you to know something. I've been doing this job for almost ten years, and I've had to deliver a lot of bad news to a lot of families. Most of them want to know the same thing you're asking me — how did it happen? Most of them end up regretting that they asked."

Tears welled up in Tasha's eyes. She wiped them away, willed herself to be strong, and held her ground. "I want to know."

Detective Marchand glanced at Detective Pirelli, who shrugged. He didn't seem as concerned as she was. "The papers are going to get hold of the story eventually, if they haven't already," he said. "She'll be reading about it and seeing it on TV for the next couple of weeks. We all will."

Tasha's father said nothing, but nodded almost imperceptibly.

Detective Marchand looked sad and tired. "Okay," she said, her voice barely a whisper. She held Tasha's eyes. "The coroner thinks the murder weapon was a knife or maybe a cleaver. Something big and sharp. Bones were chipped. Whoever attacked her, attacked her with a lot of force."

Tasha recoiled. She held up her hand to silence the detective. Tears streamed down her cheeks and this time she did nothing to stop them. Detective Marchand was right. It was better not to know everything.

That night as she lay in her bed, Tasha tried to block the detective's words from her mind. It would have been easier to forget cavities with a dentist's drill whining in her ear. Dozens of memories collided in her mind. Her mother's face, the howling of the wind and the driving rain the night she disappeared, the bitter shouting down in the kitchen. She remembered the terror that had shot through her when she finally heard the front door slam. She waited a long time for it to open again, but it didn't. There was only silence.

She knew now that there had been no silence that night, not with the wind lashing the trees outside her window, and the rain slapping against the glass. Outside, the storm had continued to rage. It was only the shouting that had stopped. Its absence had finally lured Tasha from her bed and sent her creeping down the stairs, fearful of what she would find at the bottom. She found nothing. No one. She was alone in the house.

"My daughter was only ten years old at the time," her father had told Detective Pirelli. *"I couldn't leave her alone. In fact, as I recall, I had to go upstairs and comfort her."*

But the only person within the four walls of the house that night had been Tasha.

She'd been frightened. She'd crept through every room — the kitchen, where her mother and father had been arguing, the living room, the study where her father sat each night planning menus for the days to come. No one was there. On trembling legs she'd stolen back up the stairs to her parents' room. It too was empty.

As she'd stood in the doorway, a bolt of lightning had streaked across the sky, casting the room in ghastly flickering shadows, terrifying her, bringing hot tears to her eyes. Thunder had followed the lightning like a tidal wave, overpowering, unending, crashing against the house and shaking its foundations. Tasha had dived into the bed and burrowed under the covers, comforted a little by the scent of her mother's perfume on the pillow. She'd lain there for a long time, eyes wide with fear, wishing that her parents would return.

The next thing she knew, sunlight was twinkling through the window. She'd awakened in her own room, tucked tightly under her own covers, unsure whether the events of the previous night had been nightmare or reality. Nightmare, she'd decided at last. Her parents would never leave her alone in the middle of the night.

Cheered by this conclusion — *of course* everything was just fine, *of course* her parents would never abandon her — she'd leaped from her bed and padded down the hall to their room. She'd seen the foot of the bed first, and the rumpled covers on it, and almost yelped with joy. Her parents were there. It *had* been a bad dream and nothing more.

But there was only one person in the bed. Her father sprawled flat on his back, his mouth open. He was snoring.

Tasha had felt panic, but only for a moment. Her mother was an early riser. She was probably downstairs. Maybe she was setting the table for breakfast.

But the kitchen was empty. The whole ground floor of the house was deserted. Then, as she'd turned to go back upstairs, she'd seen them — her father's shoes, standing in a puddle in the front hall.

Now Tasha lay in her bed, staring at the ceiling. Had her father forgotten that he'd gone out that night, or had he knowingly lied to the police?

The next day, Tasha didn't bother to get dressed. Her father stayed home from the restaurant, too, even though Saturday was his busiest day. For the most part he was as quiet as she was. Once or twice she heard his voice, hushed, as he spoke on the telephone. She didn't know, didn't care, who the caller was. She thought only of her mother.

* * *

"You okay?" Jace asked when he dropped by on Sunday afternoon. Tasha hadn't wanted to go downstairs to see him, but her father insisted. Jace offered her a smile, but there was so much sadness under it that it looked like a coat of paint slapped on a cracked and crumbling wall.

"I heard what happened," he said. "It was on the news."

Tasha sank down onto the couch in the living room. Detective Pirelli had been right. The media had got hold of the story. It was in the newspapers, on TV, on the radio. There was no avoiding it.

Jace sat beside her. "I'm really sorry about what happened, Tasha," he said. "I wish I could say I know how you feel, but . . . . "

31

Tasha nodded. The last time she had felt like this was a couple of weeks after her mother had left, when she'd realized that it might be a long time before she came back. She'd thought then that nothing could happen that could ever make her feel any worse. She'd been wrong. For a moment, neither she nor Jace spoke. For once the silence between them was anything but comfortable.

"I wish there was something I could do," he said at last. "I wish there was some way I could make this whole thing go away."

"You can't. Nobody can. But I guess I'll survive," she said, more to make him feel better than out of any real conviction. Life would just keep happening, but she wasn't sure she wanted it to, not if it was going to feel like this. "I'm going back to school tomorrow. We can't do anything about a funeral until . . . until the autopsy report is complete." She couldn't believe she was actually saying this. It didn't seem possible that she was now living a life that involved autopsies, the police, criminal investigations.

"I'll pick you up if you want," Jace said.

Tasha knew how much he wanted to do something for her. "That would be nice," she said. It would also be easier to walk into school with Jace than to have to do it alone. They sat side by side for a few minutes longer, then Jace put his arm around her shoulder. Tasha leaned her head against him and closed her eyes.

Going back to school the next day was one of the hardest things she'd ever done. Everyone knew what had happened. They all stared at her as she walked with Jace across the school parking lot. Kids she knew well, and others she barely knew at all, came to offer their condolences. Rick Jansen turned red in the face and could barely look at her as he told her how sorry he was to have heard what he called "the terrible news." Some kids lingered longer than necessary after delivering their sympathy, and Tasha couldn't help thinking that they were hoping for details that hadn't been included in the news reports. She wished she could stay at home forever.

* * *

"Day four," Jace said three days later. "If you can get through today, a great reward awaits you."

"It does?" Tasha was tired of being stared at. She resented that kids were talking about her. Daily news reports about her mother's murder made it impossible for her to put the whole thing out of her mind for even a few hours. But when she was with Jace she felt normal — well, as normal as possible. "What reward? Will I win a prize?"

"You bet." Jace grinned at her. "If you make it through today, I'm going to see to it that tomorrow is declared Friday."

"Big deal," Tasha said, smiling back at him, thinking she was lucky to have a friend who cared enough to try to make her feel better instead of worse. "Even if I don't make it through today, tomorrow will *still* be Friday. Just another school day."

"True. Just another school day. Followed by the most terrific evening you've had in a long, long time."

Tasha frowned. What was he talking about?

33

Jace grinned and reached into his pocket. "Ta-dah!" he said as he pulled out what looked like a pair of tickets. "The My Sanity concert! Fifth row centre."

She stared at the tickets with exaggerated suspicion. How had he managed to get hold of them?

"I thought that concert sold out a month ago," she said.

"Six weeks ago, to be exact," Jace replied.

"You've had those tickets for six weeks and you're only telling me about them now?"

"Actually, I've had them for about six days. I bought them from Sharon Wong last week."

Tasha stared. Sharon Wong . . . Last week Jace had kissed Sharon in the hallway at school.

"Her brother works for a booking agent," Jace explained. "He has access to tickets for the hottest groups around." He looked pleased with himself.

"And Sharon got the tickets for you?"

Jace shrugged. "She owed me. I put in a lot of time helping her with a computer project last term. She doesn't have what you'd call natural aptitude for computers. In return, she promised me tickets to the show of my choice. I wasn't sure she was going to be able to come through with these, though. They're worth their weight in gold. I couldn't believe it when she told me last week that she had them."

So there wasn't anything special between Jace and Sharon. It had all been about homework.

"Hey," Jace said, "is something wrong?"

"No. Nothing." He'd kissed Sharon because she'd given him a pair of tickets to the hottest concert of the year. "I think it's great."

Jace peered at her as if he were trying to read on her face what was in her heart. "I've done something wrong, haven't I? This is probably bad timing. Look, if you don't feel like going, it's no problem." He tucked the tickets back into his pocket. "It's just my lame attempt to make you feel better."

"You haven't done anything wrong," Tasha said quickly. "Sometimes I think I'd go crazy without you. You're the only person who doesn't look at me like I'm some kind of freak." Impetuously she kissed him on the cheek. He looked so surprised that she laughed for the first time in days. It felt good.

* * *

"The concert was fabulous!" Tasha raved as she and Jace headed back to his car. She skipped along beside him, her head filled with music. "Thank you, thank you, thank you."

"You should be thanking Sharon." Jace looked as delighted as she was, and had been grinning all night.

He was happy to have made her happy, Tasha thought, and that pleased her. "I'll make a point of doing that next time I see her," she promised.

They stopped for pizza, which they ate while discussing the show, then Jace drove her home. As they got close to her house Tasha began to wonder whether tonight would be the night. He'd taken her to a concert. Maybe tonight, when he dropped her off at her house, he'd kiss her. Maybe tonight he'd make the change from being her best friend to being her boyfriend. She hoped so. She yearned for it to happen. She felt herself tingle all over as he turned onto her street. Then she froze.

Jace blinked at the sight that greeted them. "There's a police car outside your house."

"Two police cars," Tasha said, amazed she could speak at all with her heart in her throat. The grey car that belonged to detectives Pirelli and Marchand sat behind a patrol car with flashing lights. What were they doing there? What had happened? Had her father been hurt?

She jumped out of Jace's car before it came to a complete stop and was halfway up the walk when the front door opened. Detective Marchand came out, followed by Tasha's father and two uniformed police officers. Detective Pirelli followed behind.

"Dad!" Tasha shouted. "Dad, what's happening?"

Leonard Scanlan, his face pale in the bright glare of the porch light, looked sadly at her. His shoulders rolled in a shrug of apology.

Tasha tried to run to him, but Detective Marchand held her back while her father continued down the walk. As he passed, Tasha saw that his hands were cuffed behind his back. "What are you doing?" she cried. "Where are you taking my father?"

"He's under arrest, Tasha," Detective Marchand said in a calm voice.

Under arrest? It wasn't possible. Tasha looked frantically toward the street. Jace had got out of his car and was watching in stunned silence as Leonard Scanlan was eased into the back of the police cruiser.

"Why did you arrest him?" Tasha demanded.

"What has he done?"

Detective Marchand turned to her. "Your father is under arrest for the murder of your mother."

Chapter Four

"If you're taking my father to the police station, I'm going too," Tasha said.

Detective Marchand opened her mouth to say something. Tasha was sure she was going to argue. Instead she said, "I think that's a good idea, Tasha. We have to ask you some questions, and it looks like no matter what happens, your father's not going to be released tonight. That means we'll need to arrange some place for you to stay."

"She can stay at my house," Jace said, stepping forward so suddenly he seemed to startle Detective Marchand. "I'll talk to my parents, Tasha, and catch up with you at the police station, okay?"

"Okay," Tasha said. She reached out and touched his hand. He held it for a moment, then, so quickly Tasha didn't have time to be surprised, he kissed her. While she watched him run back to his car, she fingered the still-warm place where his lips had brushed her skin.

She sat in silence in the back of the detectives' car. It wasn't possible, she told herself over and over again. It wasn't possible that her father had been arrested. How could anyone think that he was capable of murder?

When they finally pulled up in front of the police station Tasha saw her father being helped out of the back of the squad car. Camera flashes lit up the night as he was led through a small crowd.

"Blasted press," muttered Detective Marchand. "Let's take her around the back way, Pirelli."

For the first time in her life, Tasha entered a police station. She was surprised at how crowded and noisy it was. The place hummed with dozens of sounds — the clickety-clack of fingers on computer keyboards, the buzz of conversation and the staccato of shouting. There were people everywhere — at desks, hunkered down on uncomfortable looking chairs, squeezing past each other on the way in, or the way out. If the station was this busy at nearly midnight, she thought, she could only imagine how congested it might be during the day.

"This way," Detective Marchand said, laying a hand on Tasha's shoulder to guide her toward a flight of stairs. At the top she directed Tasha to a small room that seemed crowded by the few pieces of furniture it contained: a scarred table and four battered chairs. "I'll be right back."

"Where's my father?"

"He's being processed."

"I want to see him."

"I'll see what I can do," the detective said. "I promise. But first you and I have to talk. Just stay here. I'll be back in a minute."

Tasha sat and stared down at the floor, which was layered with grime. Detective Marchand returned a few minutes later, accompanied by a steely-haired woman in a floral print dress.

"This is Mrs. Evans," Detective Marchand said. "She's a child welfare worker. She's going to sit in on our conversation, okay, Tasha?"

Tasha looked at the woman, who smiled back at her. "I want to see my father," she said.

"We'll see what we can do," Mrs. Evans said. "But first the police want to ask you some questions."

"We're going to videotape our conversation, all right, Tasha?" Detective Marchand asked.

"Why?"

"You're a minor. We want to tape our conversation just so that everyone can see that there's no coercion here, that you're talking to me because you want to. Mrs. Evans is here to ensure that. Okay?"

"My father didn't do anything," Tasha snapped.

"Is it okay if we tape this, Tasha?" Detective Marchand repeated.

Still angry, Tasha nodded.

"Okay," Detective Marchand said. She glanced for a moment at the mirror that took up almost all of one wall. Tasha realized that it must be one-way glass. Not only was she being videotaped, she was being watched.

"Look at me, Tasha," Detective Marchand said, quietly but firmly. Tasha forced herself to look directly into the purple-flecked eyes. "I have to ask you some questions, Tasha, and it's very important that you answer them truthfully."

Tasha felt the heat rise in her cheeks. Did Detective Marchand think she was going to lie? Is that the kind of person she thought Tasha was?

Detective Marchand looked evenly at her for a few moments, then said, "I want you to tell me everything you can remember about the night your mother disappeared."

Tasha's eyes shifted to the floor again, this time so the detective couldn't see how she was struggling to decide what to do. Her father had told the police he'd been home all night. Tasha knew it wasn't true, but if she told Detective Marchand her father had lied, it could only make things worse for him.

"Your father said that he and your mother had an argument that night," Detective Marchand prompted. "Do you remember that, Tasha? Did you hear them fighting?"

"I was upstairs in my room," Tasha said. "In bed."

"Look at me, Tasha."

Reluctantly Tasha looked up.

"Did you hear your parents arguing?"

Tasha nodded.

"Do you know what they were arguing about?"

"No," she said. Then, "Well, sort of. They . . . they fought a lot, about all kinds of things." Whenever they raised their voices she would start to tremble, afraid of what might happen. "I think my mother was angry about the Café. She said . . . she said it was the only thing my father cared about. She said she was glad she was out of it, and that she couldn't wait to go away." As Tasha spoke, she could hear their loud, sharp exchange. "I was sure they were going to get a divorce."

"Do you remember anything else they said to each other that night?"

"No." What good would it do to tell the detective that Tasha's mother resented her, that she hated being tied down by a child?

"After they finished arguing, what happened?"

"My mother left."

"Did you see or hear her leave?"

Panic fluttered in Tasha's chest. She would have to be very careful about what she said next. "I heard the front door open, and then slam shut."

"And your mother left?"

"I . . . I guess so."

"Did you see her go?"

Tasha shook her head.

"What about your father?"

Tasha bit her lip.

"Tasha? What did your father do after your mother left?"

He'd told the police he'd gone upstairs to comfort her, but he hadn't. She hadn't seen him again until the next morning, and then she'd also seen his wet shoes. But he must have had a reason for saying what he had. Or maybe he'd been so upset that he'd forgotten what had really happened that night. Either way, Detective Marchand would only become more suspicious if Tasha told what she remembered.

"Tasha?"

The police thought her father was guilty of murder. If she told them that he'd lied about being home, or if they believed he had lied to them when in fact he'd only forgotten what had happened, they'd be more convinced than ever.

"Tasha, you promised to tell me everything."

"My father isn't a murderer," Tasha insisted. "He loved my mother. They argued a lot, but he would never have done anything to hurt her."

"If we're going to sort out this mess, Tasha, we have to know *exactly* what happened. If you want to help your father, you have to tell the truth."

She didn't see how her father could benefit by her telling this particular piece of truth.

"You won't help him by lying, Tasha."

Tasha felt the detective's eyes on her, but didn't have the courage to meet her gaze.

"For the last time, Tasha. Did your father come up and talk to you after your mother left the house?"

What should she do? Lie? Tell the detective something was true when it wasn't? Or should she tell what she really remembered? Wasn't that always the best way, wasn't honesty always the best policy?

"No," Tasha cried at last. "No, he didn't. They left me all alone in the house. I heard the door slam and I got up to see what was happening and there was no one there. No one at all."

Half an hour later Tasha sat beside Mrs. Evans on a bench in a crowded hallway, waiting for Detective Marchand. Tears blurred her vision. She wiped them away as fast as they appeared, determined to keep control of her emotions for as long as she sat on public display. The fact was, though, that things looked bad for her father, and not just because of what she had told Detective Marchand. From the questions she'd been asked she was able to piece together that the police had already canvassed the Scanlans' old neighbours. One of them remembered seeing Leonard Scanlan leave the house the night of her mother's disappearance.

"That's impossible," Tasha had told Detective Marchand when she mentioned it. "It happened five *years* ago. *I* remember that night because it was the night my mother left. But how could anyone else be so sure that they saw my father do anything on a specific night over five years ago?"

"It was the night Hurricane Bradley went through here," Detective Marchand reminded her. "A tree came down in the man's front yard and smashed his front window."

She was referring to Mr. Danvers, Tasha realized. He'd lived right across the street from their old house.

"He was out in the storm, trying to nail plywood over the window to keep the wind and rain from coming in. He says he remembers that your father was out that night because he called to him to ask for help. Your father didn't stop."

There could be dozens of reasons why her father had gone out that night, Tasha had argued. And anyway, leaving the house didn't make him a murderer. "What about those letters my mother wrote to us?" she asked.

"Ah, the letters." Detective Marchand didn't look very happy. "You saw those letters, didn't you, Tasha?"

"Yes," she said. "They were on plain white paper,

neatly — " She had been going to say that they were neatly typed, but no sooner had she thought the words than she knew something was wrong, and wondered why it had never occurred to her before. Not only was her mother not very good at typing, she hated doing it. Whenever she made up the menus for the Café, she refused to work at a computer. "I can write it out faster and neater by hand," she always said. She was so reluctant to sit in front of a keyboard that she used to pay to have her term papers typed. How likely was it that she would sit down in Vancouver and type letters to Tasha and her father? Wouldn't she have written them by hand instead?

"Your father promised to keep them for you, didn't he?" Detective Marchand had asked her.

Tasha nodded.

"But he didn't, did he? He destroyed them, isn't that right?"

Again Tasha nodded. She still didn't understand why he'd done that. Tasha had cried each time a letter arrived, partly because she was so thrilled that her mother had remembered her, and partly because each letter was a reminder of her mother's continuing absence. She'd wanted to hold the letters, to smell them and touch them and imagine her mother folding them and putting them into their envelopes. Her father said he understood how she felt, but that she'd wear them out if she kept taking them out of the envelopes and reading them. He said he'd keep them safe for her. And then he'd destroyed them. It didn't make sense.

Still, even that didn't prove anything. Her father

had been as devastated as Tasha by Catherine Scanlan's disappearance. Maybe more so. He had probably burned the letters out of anger or sadness.

But there was something else Tasha found out, something that, when added to all the other facts, made it all look worse.

"When your mother and father got married," Detective Marchand had told her, "your grandfather made them joint owners of the Fireside Café. Six weeks before your mother disappeared, she sold her share of the Café to your father. Your father said she wanted the money to finance a trip around the world." She had paused, and Tasha sensed the worst part was about to come. "Do you remember when your father finally sold the Café?"

"Sure. He sold it just after . . . " Just after her mother had disappeared. Tasha stared at the detective. "He was *hurt* when she left. He didn't want to be reminded of her day after day." It made sense. After her mother had gone, Tasha didn't like to think of the Fireside Café either. In fact, she hadn't set foot in the place ever again in case old memories would be stirred up by its smells and sights.

"He sold it for much less than it was worth," Detective Marchand had said. "That doesn't look good, Tasha. People might think he sold it at such a low price because he was desperate to get rid of it. Because of what was in the basement."

"But . . . No, that doesn't make sense. If my father wanted to keep a body buried down there then he would have held *onto* the place, not sold it," Tasha had argued. Then she remembered what her father had said to Denny. He hadn't wanted the Café to be demolished. He'd said, "If anyone should be upset about the Fireside Café being torn down, it should be me." Tasha had thought he meant he was sad to see the end of a place with so much tradition and so many personal memories attached to it. Maybe that wasn't what he meant at all . . . .

Tasha sat now on the bench, numbed by all she had learned. What was going to happen now?

"Tasha?"

She looked around at the sound of Jace's voice. Relief flickered in his dark eyes. Standing behind him was his father. Sanjit Bhupal was a little shorter than his son. Tasha stood up as he walked over to greet her, which he did gravely.

"How are you holding up, Natasha?" he asked.

"Okay, I guess."

"Jason has told me everything," he said. "Who's in charge around here? Who can I talk to?"

Mrs. Evans stood up and introduced herself.

"My son is a close friend of Natasha's," he said. "We'd like her to stay with us for the night, with her father's permission. She has no relatives living close by."

While Mrs. Evans and Mr. Bhupal discussed the matter, Jace said, "Tasha, are you okay? What's going on?"

"They think he did it," Tasha said, shaking her head in disbelief. "They really think my father murdered my mother."

Jace said nothing, but took one of her hands and squeezed it.

Mrs. Evans walked away for a moment. When she returned, Detective Marchand was with her.

"Can I stay with the Bhupals?" Tasha asked Mrs. Evans.

"If it's all right with your father," she said.

"Why don't you ask him?" Detective Marchand said.

Ask him? Tasha's heart raced. "Can I see him?"

"Just for a minute," Detective Marchand said.

"We'll wait for you here," Jace said. "Won't we, Dad?"

* * *

Leonard Scanlan was sitting on a hard-backed chair on the far side of a wall of thick glass. He held a telephone receiver in his hand, and Tasha saw that she'd have to pick up another receiver on her side of the glass to be able to speak to him. His face looked pale with worry and exhaustion. She wondered what he was thinking — that his arrest was a gigantic mistake, or that he'd finally been discovered?

She felt ashamed at that last thought, but no matter how hard she tried, she couldn't shake it. Things did look bad.

Her fingers trembled as she lifted the receiver off its hook. When at last she pressed it to her ear, she said, "Are you okay, Dad?"

"About as well as can be expected," he said. "They let me call a lawyer. His name is Roger Brubaker. He'll probably want to talk to you at some point. I asked him to get in touch with your Aunt Cynthia and see if she could come and stay with you until this mess is cleared up."

"Aunt Cynthia?" Tasha hadn't seen her aunt since long before her mother's disappearance.

She'd always had the impression that her mother and Aunt Cynthia didn't get along, although she didn't know why.

"I hope Cynthia can get here some time tomorrow. I don't know what we can do about tonight, Tash. Maybe Mr. Brubaker . . . "

"It's okay. The Bhupals have asked me to stay with them. We can let Aunt Cynthia know. Mr. Bhupal and Jace are waiting for me outside."

Her father sank back in his chair. He almost smiled. "Good," he said. "I was so worried."

He was worried about *that*? "I'm going to be fine, Dad. You don't have to worry about me. It's you . . . " What could she say?

"I don't know what they've told you, Tasha. But I want you to know from me that I didn't do it. I would *never* have hurt your mother. You have to believe me, Tasha."

"I do." She hoped he didn't notice the uncertainty in her voice. She wished she could reach through the glass and hug him, and at the same time, she was almost glad that she couldn't.

Chapter Five

Mrs. Bhupal was small and blonde, with clear green eyes and a faint Scottish accent that lingered from her childhood in Edinburgh. She swung open the front door while Mr. Bhupal was still fumbling for his keys. She must have been watching for them, Tasha realized. She welcomed Tasha with a hug and asked whether she wanted anything to eat.

"No, thank you," Tasha said. She was desperately tired. It was well past midnight, and felt as if it had been the longest day of her life.

"Why don't I show you to your room?" Mrs. Bhupal said. She led Tasha upstairs and into a room with floral wallpaper and a pale pink ceiling. A fold-out couch was already made up, and clean towels had been set out in the adjoining bathroom. Mrs. Bhupal opened the closet and brought out a nightie. "You can wear this tonight, dear," she said. "And don't worry about anything. You just get up whenever you want, and we'll take it from there."

Tasha thanked her and, after Mrs. Bhupal had left the room, sank down onto the fold-out bed. Her father was in jail. The grim-faced police seemed deadly serious about keeping him there. And her mother — tears welled up in her eyes and a sob escaped her — her mother was dead. Her whole life had been turned upside down, and now it looked like it was in for a good, hard shaking before things settled again. And there was no guarantee that they'd settle back to the way they were before the wrecking ball had slammed into the old stone walls of the Fireside Café. That same wrecking ball had slammed right into her life, too.

Someone knocked gently on the door. Tasha quickly wiped her tears.

"Tash?"

It was Jace.

"Come in," she said.

Jace poked his head into the room. "I just wanted to make sure you're okay." He peered at her, and offered her a wan smile. "I guess that sounds pretty lame under the circumstances."

Tasha shook her head. Jace could probably tell she'd been crying. "It's so weird," she said. "I can't believe this is happening. I keep thinking I'm going to wake up, or that the movie's going to end."

He sat down beside her. "I wish I could tell you I know exactly how you feel," he said, "but this is totally out of my league."

"It's not exactly an average day for me, either," Tasha said. She looked at Jace's clear, smooth face, his small, sharp nose, his dark brown eyes. "What if they're right?" she said. "What if he really did it?"

Jace seemed startled by the question. "You don't really believe that, do you?"

"I don't know *what* to believe." She told Jace everything that Detective Marchand had said, and everything she knew herself.

He shook his head slowly. "But this is your father we're talking about, Tasha. He's a cook, not a killer."

Tasha would have given anything to feel as sure as Jace sounded.

* * *

She woke to the sound of a car door slamming and was surprised, when she glanced at her watch, to see that it was nearly three o'clock. Three in the afternoon, she realized, for the sun was streaming through the window. She had slept more than half the day away.

She got up, washed and dressed quickly, and was making the bed when Mrs. Bhupal knocked on the door.

"Your aunt is here, Tasha," she said.

Aunt Cynthia was a taller, thinner, blonde version of Tasha's mother. The family resemblance, manifested in penetrating hazel eyes, a wide mouth, and cascades of thick wavy hair, was so strong that no one who knew one sister would have had any trouble picking the other one out of a line–up. There were dark circles under Aunt Cynthia's eyes, and her hair needed a good brushing. She must not have had much sleep, Tasha realized. To get here from Washington State she must have boarded a plane early in the morning — right after finding out about her sister's murder.

"I have a taxi waiting," she said to Tasha. "Let's get your things together." She spoke as if Tasha were a four-year-old who needed help gathering up her toys.

"I don't have any things," Tasha said stiffly. She thanked Mrs. Bhupal for her hospitality, then followed her aunt to the taxi.

"You've sure grown," Aunt Cynthia said on the way home. "What are you now, fourteen?"

"Fifteen," Tasha said. "Almost sixteen."

Aunt Cynthia shook her head. "Sixteen," she sighed. "I remember sixteen. The golden age. How are you holding up?"

"Okay, I guess."

"Poor Cathy," Aunt Cynthia said. "I always had the feeling that your father was hiding something from me."

Tasha stared at her aunt. "What are you saying? Are you saying you think my father did it?"

Aunt Cynthia's cheeks turned red. "Well, I . . . Tasha, he *was* arrested. Surely the police — "

"I don't know why my father asked you to come here," Tasha snapped. "You're not even on his side. You've already made up your mind that he's guilty." She slouched in her seat and didn't say another word all the way home.

* * *

"I know you're angry with me," Aunt Cynthia said as she set a plate of spaghetti in front of Tasha. For an hour she had chattered non-stop while she prepared the meal, pretending she hadn't said what she had in the taxi, telling Tasha more than anyone could ever want to know about the little diner that

53

she managed in Washington.

Tasha had said little in response, and now Aunt Cynthia was trying to clear the air.

"The truth is, your father and I never got along very well. But I guess that's no secret, is it?"

"I thought it was my mother you didn't get along with," Tasha said. "I didn't realize it was the whole family."

"Your mother and I got along fine," Aunt Cynthia said. "I miss . . . I missed her terribly, and then to hear that she'd been . . . " Her cheeks were flushed, and she held herself stiff. "Anyway, it wasn't her fault that Daddy handed the Fireside Café over to her and your father lock, stock and barrel. But how do you think that made *me* feel? Catherine wasn't the only cook in the family. She never even wanted to go into the restaurant business. She only agreed to it because your father wanted it so much, and she was crazy in love with him. *I'm* the one who graduated from the Cordon Bleu in Paris. Did you know that? But Cathy was always Daddy's favourite, and he really liked Leonard too. So when he was ready to retire he signed the Café over to them. He never even asked me what I wanted or whether I'd be interested."

Tasha was astonished by her aunt's bitterness. She spoke as if the blow to her pride had been inflicted hours ago, instead of years ago.

"Why didn't you just tell your father how you felt? Why did you take it out on my mother?"

"I did no such thing," Aunt Cynthia said.

"You two used to fight all the time."

"We did not."

"Sure you did. I used to hear you every time you came to visit."

Aunt Cynthia pushed her spaghetti around her plate for a little while. Then she laid her fork aside.

"We didn't fight *all* the time," she began. "You're probably just remembering the last time I was here. Boy, did we go at it then. That's when I found out that Cathy had sold her half of the Café to your father, making him sole owner. I guess that was a month or so before she . . . before she disappeared. It never even occurred to her to offer to sell her half to me. And she *knew* how I felt about the Café. She knew I would have done anything for a chance to run it." She shook her head, as if to chase away her mounting anger. "The Café had been in our family for over sixty years. Your great-grandfather started the place. And your mother just sold it to your father as if it were an old piece of furniture she didn't want any more, as if it had no special meaning. She never even thought about me. And then, soon after . . . " Her voice trailed off. She stabbed at her spaghetti. "Your father sold the place, just like that. He didn't tell me he'd done it until months later, when it was too late for me to do anything about it. I would have taken the place off his hands. I would have been proud to run the Fireside Café. But nobody gave me a chance."

Tasha stared at her aunt in amazement. "I had no idea."

Aunt Cynthia shrugged. "There's no reason you should have," she said. "You were just a kid."

They sat opposite each other at the kitchen table, both of them poking at their food, neither of them eating. Finally Tasha asked, "Do you think my father did it?"

Aunt Cynthia looked up, startled.

"Tasha — "

"You don't know what it's like," Tasha said. "People talk about it behind my back, then clam up when I'm around. They've all made up their minds one way or the other. Mostly the other. But you know my father. You know what kind of a person he is. What do you think?"

Aunt Cynthia fiddled with her glass of water. "I think questions like that are best left to experts," she said. "That's what police and lawyers are for, to find out what really happened, who really did what."

Tasha stared at her aunt for a moment. A hard knot formed in the pit of her stomach.

"You said in the taxi that you always thought my father was hiding something from you," she said. "What did you mean?"

"Why don't we change the subject?" Aunt Cynthia said. "We have a lot of catching up to do. The last time I saw you, you were a whole lot shorter and a whole lot younger. And now, well, you're sixteen."

"Fifteen," Tasha said.

Aunt Cynthia smiled. Her lips quivered, as if they were straining to hold the expression. "Fifteen," she said. "I stand corrected."

Tasha's hand slammed so hard against the tabletop that the plates and glasses jumped. "Tell me what you meant! Be straight with me. Is that asking so much?"

Aunt Cynthia stared at her across the dinner

table. She reached for her glass of ice water and sipped it. As she set the glass back on the table she said, "We have to be together for a while, Tasha. It could be weeks, maybe longer. I think it would be best for both of us if we tried not to talk about what's happened, if we concentrated instead on trying to live as normally as possible."

Tasha was on her feet before her aunt stopped talking. "If you thought he was innocent, you would have said so," she cried. "You're avoiding giving me an answer because you know it's something I don't want to hear."

"Tasha — "

"Am I wrong?" Tasha shouted. She felt betrayed by her own aunt, her mother's own sister. "If I'm wrong, then tell me. Say, 'You're wrong, Tasha, I believe with my whole heart that your father is innocent.' Go ahead, say it!"

Aunt Cynthia stared at her in stunned silence.

Tasha glared back. Then she turned and fled from the house.

* * *

"Jason is out in the garage," Mr. Bhupal said, scrutinizing Tasha, making her feel self-conscious. She was sure her eyes were red and swollen. With her luck, her cheeks were probably smudged where she'd wiped at her tears. She'd worked hard at not crying, without success. She hated looking pathetic all the time. But whenever she thought things were as bad as they could get, they got worse. If Aunt Cynthia didn't believe her father was innocent, what chance was there that anyone else would? What chance was there that he really was innocent?

"Is everything okay, Tasha?" Mr. Bhupal asked.

"Fine," Tasha said. Her voice cracked on the word, and she felt compelled to smile so he'd believe her. "I'm fine, really, Mr. Bhupal. Thanks."

She was relieved when he went back inside. She hurried to the garage at the back of the property, and rapped on the small side door before pushing it open. Jace was sitting at a work bench, fiddling with a little metal box. A laptop computer sat open at his elbow. He smiled at her when she came in.

"Pull up a stool," he said. When she sat down beside him, he studied her carefully. "Been crying, huh?" he said.

She nodded and then quickly changed the subject so she wouldn't start blubbering all over again. "What are you working on?" she asked. With Jace, if it wasn't something to do with computers, it was something electronic. He loved gadgets.

"I'm modifying this tracking device for my grandmother."

Tasha frowned. "Why does your grandmother need a tracking device?"

"She has her suspicions about Charlie."

"Charlie?"

"Her cat. Apparently he leads a secret life."

When Tasha shook her head in confusion, he explained. "Charlie likes to prowl around all night. But he's getting old, and my grandmother worries about him. You know, what if he gets lost? What if he has some kind of accident and she has no idea where he is? That kind of thing."

"So you made her a tracking device?"

"I bought the tracking device. I modified it to

58

interface with my grandmother's computer — "

"Your grandmother has a computer?"

Jace grinned. "Sure," he said. "After all, she's *my* grandmother. The way I have it rigged up, when this little gizmo is attached to Charlie's collar, it will send out a signal that Grandma can track on her computer. Look." He waved her closer. "What do you see?"

She peered at the computer screen. "Looks like a map of the city."

"Actually," Jace said, "it's a map of the neighbourhood. Watch." He pushed the arrow right key, and the map shifted to the left. "I've got the whole city on there, compliments of the Planning Department — well, compliments of Dad, actually. Okay, now watch that screen," he said as he darted for the door.

"Hey, where are you going?"

"Watch the screen, the little blip."

Tasha watched as Jace disappeared out of the garage. The little blip ran down Dunlop Street, where Jace lived, turned east on Jamieson, then south on Linders, and north back onto Dunlop. A few minutes later, Jace was back in the garage, panting for breath.

"Do you know where I went?" he asked.

Tasha smiled. "Around the block." Then she added, "This is great."

Jace beamed. "With this, my grandmother can keep tabs on exactly where Charlie is, within a two-kilometre radius of her house. Actually, this thing can track ten times that distance. But Grandma doesn't need that much range. Charlie's eight years old. How far can he go?"

Tasha shrugged. "I don't know much about cats." In fact, she knew nothing at all.

All of a sudden, the screen went dark. "Oh-oh," Jace said.

"What happened?"

"It crashed." He shook his head. "Slight glitch. I'm not sure whether it's the map or the tracking device that's causing the problem." He sat down again and started to fiddle with the device.

Tasha watched him for a few minutes, then said, "Is it okay if I talk while you work?"

He flashed her a smile. "Sure," he said. "You shouldn't even have to ask."

That made her feel a little better, and she relaxed as she began to tell him what her aunt had said.

When she'd finished, Jace said, "If you ask me, it's a good thing she's here."

"Good? What's good about it? Didn't you hear what I said? She thinks my father is guilty."

"It sounds to me like your aunt has helped you finally make up your mind about your dad. As a matter of fact, it sounds like you agree with me."

"What do you mean?"

"Your dad's innocent, Tasha."

She stared at him. "You say that like it's a fact."

"Isn't it?"

"But what about all the other stuff I told you? What about him going out that night? What about him selling the Café in a hurry for less than it was worth?"

Jace shrugged. "There must be logical explanations for those things."

"How do you know?"

"Has your dad ever hurt anyone that you know of?"

"No."

"Did he ever hit your mom when they used to fight?"

"No."

"I like your dad. He's a nice guy and a great cook. He's not a murderer."

"But the police — "

" — are doing everything they can to hang this murder on him, and I'm sure the crown attorney's office is right there with them. *And* the press. I don't think there are many people on your father's side."

Tasha's mind raced. She didn't want to believe her father was guilty. But all the facts of the case were against him. Still, Jace was right. She knew it in her heart. Her father *was* a good man. When he and her mother used to fight, it was usually because she had started it, not him. And even though he could get so angry that he lost his temper, she had never seen him actually become physical. He had never raised a hand against her, or anyone else that Tasha could remember. He'd never even spanked her. But . . . "If the police are so convinced my father's the murderer," she said, "then they aren't going to spend much time looking for whoever the real murderer is."

Jace nodded.

"Which means," Tasha said, thinking it through as she formed the words, "that someone is going to have to show them they're wrong."

Chapter Six

"Where have you been?" Aunt Cynthia demanded, breathless, when she opened the front door.

Tasha guessed that her aunt had been watching for her at the window. "Out," she said. She was still angry with her aunt and wished she had never bothered to fly in from Washington. She wished she could stay with the Bhupals instead.

"I was worried."

Who cares? Tasha wanted to snarl. Instead she said, "I can take care of myself."

"I don't doubt that," Aunt Cynthia replied. "You're a lot like your mother — very strong-willed." She offered a tentative smile, but Tasha didn't return it. Aunt Cynthia sighed and shook her head. "I know you're mad at me," she said, "and I'm sorry. It's just that — "

"Just that *what*?" Tasha said. "Just that you think my father is a murderer?"

Aunt Cynthia was silent for a few moments.

Slowly she shook her head. "Maybe Cathy and I weren't as close as some sisters," she said. "But we always kept in touch. *Always*." She peered at Tasha, and seemed to be trying to make up her mind about something. "I talked to your father a few months after your mother . . . after she left him. I wanted to know where she was. He told me he'd received a few letters from Vancouver. Well, I tried to trace her there. Nothing. But when I told him, he didn't seem to care. She was probably gallivanting around the world, he said. He implied it was just like her to think only about herself." Tears clouded her eyes. "But it *wasn't*, Tasha. It wasn't like Cathy at all. Whatever else she was, she wasn't so callous that she'd leave her family, that she'd never contact them again. Your father must have known that."

"So you think he was lying to you?" Tasha said.

"I can't help the way I feel."

"Neither can I," Tasha said. There had to be a reason why her father had said what he had to Aunt Cynthia. Probably he believed it. Maybe to him, his wife's leaving was such a cruel act he couldn't bring himself to try to find her. "If you have the right to think what you want, so do I. And I think — no, I *know* — that my father is innocent. I don't care that I'm probably the only person who believes it — " She paused and thought about Jace. "Well, I'm half of the people who believe it. It's true, and I plan to do everything I can to prove it."

Aunt Cynthia's hazel eyes widened. "Tasha, this is a police matter — "

"The police think they've got the case solved. Now that they've made an arrest, I bet they aren't even investigating any other possibilities. They're concentrating on doing everything they can to get Dad convicted. Nobody's trying to prove he's innocent. Nobody except me and Jace."

"Tasha, wait. Your father's lawyer will be challenging any of the evidence that he can — "

"You can say what you want, Aunt Cynthia, but you can't stop me. If you don't like that, fine. You can go back home to Washington. I can look after myself."

Aunt Cynthia shook her head, and backed away as if in surrender.

* * *

The next day was Sunday. Tasha got up early and hurried over to Jace's house. She found him in the garage.

"I've been thinking about this all night," she blurted. "If we're starting from the premise that my father didn't do it, then we have to believe that someone else did. If we're going to find out who that person is, we have to concentrate on what happened to my mother after she left the house that night — where she went, who she might have seen, all of that."

"Sounds reasonable," Jace said. He was still fiddling with the homing device for his grandmother's cat, and kept glancing at the screen of his laptop.

"Yeah, except how do we do that? Where do we start?"

"I guess we start with what we know. Which is . . . " Jace thought a moment, then peered at her. "What exactly do we know?"

"We know that my mother left the house very late on the night of a big storm."

"Do you have any idea what time?"

"About ten-thirty, I think. Maybe a little later. And we know that she didn't take the car because the police say my father went out in the car later that night."

"So she must have taken a taxi. Or someone gave her a lift."

Tasha shook her head in exasperation. "Either way, it's not much help. If someone gave her a lift, how could we ever find out who that person was? If she took a taxi, what are the chances that we'd be able to find out which cab company, and then find the driver — assuming he's still working there — who might remember picking her up over five years ago? The odds against it have to be a million to one."

Jace shrugged. "Let's set that aside for now and focus on what *else* we know."

"Not much." Tasha was starting to feel discouraged. This was going to be impossible. She and Jace weren't detectives.

"One thing we do know," Jace said, his eyes fixed firmly on her, "is where she ended up."

Tasha winced at the images stirred by his words — a dark basement, multiple wounds, her mother's long chestnut hair.

"I'm sorry, Tash," he said. "But if we're going to do something about this, we have to be able to talk about it."

"I know." She had to struggle to get the words out over the lump in her throat. "It's okay." She drew in a deep breath and met his gaze head on.

"What else do we know? That she went to the Fireside Café sometime that night. Either she went there of her own accord, or someone took her there against her will. Those are the only two choices."

"Maybe someone who was at the Café remembers seeing her. Would the place still have been open at ten-thirty?"

Tasha nodded. "It was open until one in the morning seven days a week."

"Then someone must have seen her. Someone on staff, maybe." He gave her an inquiring look. "I don't suppose you know who was working there at the time, do you?"

"Mr. Horstbueller."

"Horst-who?"

"Horst*bueller*." She spelled the name for Jace. "He managed the Café for my parents after my mother went back to school. Evart Horstbueller. Now there's a name you don't forget. I'm pretty sure he would have been there. My father always said he ran like a Swiss clock, which used to make my mother laugh. She always said the same thing: Evart is Dutch, he's not Swiss." As she spoke, she heard her mother's laughter. If she let herself, she'd start to cry again. But she made herself plow on. Crying wasn't going to help her father. Logic and determination were. "He used to arrive at the restaurant at ten o'clock every morning, and he always stayed until closing."

"Okay," Jace said. "So all we have to do is find this Evart Horstbueller. How hard can that be? Stay here. I'll be right back." He darted out of the garage and returned a few minutes later with a phone book, two glasses of milk, and a plate of warm bread spread with jam. "Freshly made," he said. "Mom got a breadmaker for her birthday. Every night before she goes to bed she dumps in all the ingredients, and every morning I wake up to a house that smells like the inside of a bakery. Have some."

Tasha picked at a piece. She wasn't really hungry.

"Okay, Horst . . . " Jace finished off a slice of bread and jam while he thumbed through the phone book. "Horst . . . Horsten . . . " He made a sour face. "There aren't any Horstbuellers."

"Are you sure?" Tasha slid the book away from him. "Maybe you're spelling it wrong." She ran her finger down the columns of type. Jace was right. No Horstbuellers. "He must have moved." Then a horrible thought occurred to her. "Maybe he died. He was an old man. In his fifties, I think." She slumped into her chair. "Now what?"

"Who else worked at the Café?"

Tasha shook her head. Then it struck her. "Jace! You know how when you go to a doctor's or dentist's office and they have those certificates on the wall?" she said, excited now, sure she had found a key. "My dentist has one. It proves he's a real dentist. It's like a license and it's issued by the dentists' college or something."

Jace looked puzzled. "Yeah?"

"Well, suppose you were a licensed dentist and you moved. Wouldn't the dentists' college have to keep track of where you went? Isn't that part of their job?"

"I suppose so, but — "

"Mr. Horstbueller had a certificate on the wall above his desk. It was framed and had one of those gold stickers on it, you know, like the Good House-keeping seal of approval. I remember because when I saw it, I thought he was a doctor. But it wasn't that. It was a certificate from some restaurant association."

Jace looked impressed. "Sure," he said. "Sure, that makes sense. If this Mr. Horstbueller is working in a restaurant somewhere else, or if he's retired, they might know where he is."

"Exactly," Tasha said.

Jace was already thumbing through the phone book. "Here it is," he said. "National Restaurant Association. They have an office right downtown. Come on."

"We're going downtown?"

"No, we're going inside. We're going to call them."

"And tell them what?"

That stopped him short. He thought a moment, then brightened. "That we're opening a new restaurant," he said, "and that we want to locate the famous restaurateur Evart Horstbueller so we can offer him a job."

"Not bad," Tasha laughed.

Jace pitched his voice deeper than usual and tried to sound convincing in the role of restaurant entrepreneur. But it got him nowhere. "They say they don't know what happened to him," he said when he hung up the phone. "His membership in the association lapsed about five years ago — about the same time your mother disappeared."

"Which puts us back at square one. Unless . . ." Maybe there was something else they could do, some other trail they could follow that might give them a lead.

"Unless what?" Jace said.

"My father kept a bunch of old files from the restaurant. I remember asking him once why he didn't throw them out, and he said he had to keep them just in case. Something to do with taxes, I think. Maybe there's some information in those files about people who used to work at the restaurant. There was this guy, Enrico something. He was a waiter back when I was a kid. I'm sure he was there at the same time Mr. Horstbueller was. Maybe we can find his name in Dad's records. He might know something. Maybe he was working that night. Or maybe he knows where we can find Mr. Horstbueller."

"Sounds like a plan," Jace said. "Where are these records?"

"In our basement."

Aunt Cynthia was still asleep when Tasha and Jace let themselves into Tasha's house and disappeared into the basement. Tasha led the way into the back where the furnace and the washing machine were. In one corner stood a four-drawer filing cabinet.

"The records are in there," Tasha said. She pulled open the top drawer and flipped through the many file folders inside, each one neatly labelled. They were all recent, all related to the Lenny and Denny restaurants that her father and Denny Durant owned. She tried the next drawer. It, too, was full of Lenny and Denny files. She began to feel uneasy.

What if her father had got rid of all of his old records?

The next drawer yielded nothing of value either. Tasha's hand trembled as she reached to pull open the last drawer. If there were no Fireside Café files in this drawer, that would mean either that her father had thrown out everything related to the past, or had handed all his files over to the new owner. She held her breath as she yanked the drawer open. Behind her, Jace was unusually quiet. She imagined him holding his breath along with her.

She worked her way through the file folders. At last! Here were the Fireside Café records. Old tax returns. Old medical and dental claim records. What was this? A file with no label on it. Frowning, Tasha pulled it out and yelped with surprise when a bunch of photographs spilled out onto the floor. She stood, paralysed, while Jace stooped to pick them up.

"Hey," he said, "hey, is this — "

"My mother," Tasha said. She took the photographs from him gently, almost reverently. The only picture of her mother that she'd seen in the last five years was the one in the little silver frame on her bedside table. It showed Tasha, age three, sitting on her mother's knee, both of them in navy blue velvet dresses with white lace collars, both of them smiling into the camera.

"Your mother sure was pretty," Jace said. "You look a lot like her."

Tasha's hands trembled as she sorted through them. Jace was right. Her mother was beautiful. Her smile electrified Tasha. Suddenly she was a little girl again, giggling at the funny voices her mother made as she read picture books to her, laughing gleefully as she and her mother tickled each other, swinging down the street with her mother as snow-flakes settled on their hair. She had to bite her lower lip to keep from bursting into tears. When she spoke, her voice quavered. "I thought he'd thrown these out," she said. "They just disappeared."

She set the photos back into the file folder and put the folder on top of the filing cabinet before kneeling again to continue through the files. What was this? Employment application forms and, stapled to them, employment résumés and hand-scrawled notes in what Tasha recognized as her father's handwriting.

"I think this is it," she said. Her hands trembled as she worked past the application for Mr. Horstbueller. There were several names she didn't recognize — a bus boy, a kitchen helper — then, suddenly, Enrico Zapata. "This is him," she cried. "This is the Enrico who worked at the restaurant when Mr. Horstbueller was there."

"Is there an address?"

"An address *and* a phone number." Tasha put the rest of the papers back into the file and closed the drawer. Taking the photographs and Enrico Zapata's file, she said, "Let's call him."

Minutes later Tasha's exhilaration had evaporated. Her shoulders sagged as she dropped the receiver back onto its cradle. "That number is no longer in service," she said, echoing the voice she had just heard.

Jace didn't look nearly as disappointed as Tasha. He smiled at her and said, in a voice full of bluster, "Stand back and prepare to be dazzled as I put my superior research skills into action."

While Tasha wondered what he planned to do, he reached for the telephone directory, flipped to the back of it, and started to mutter, "Zapata . . . Zapata."

Despite herself she started to laugh. "Anyone could have done that," she said.

"Ah, but anyone didn't." He grinned at her. "Well, we've got seven Zapatas, none of them E. Zapata. Then we've got one Zapata's Pizza and Wings. Here goes nothing." He picked up the receiver.

"What are you going to do?" Tasha said.

"Start calling Zapatas."

"But you said — "

"Maybe one of these Zapatas is related to the Zapata we're looking for. Or maybe Enrico is his middle name and he's listed under his first initial."

"Or maybe he's moved out of town."

"We'll never know if we don't give it a shot," Jace said. He started dialling. Tasha sat crosslegged on the floor, watching him, while he repeated a series of questions so often they began to sound scripted. "May I please speak with Mr. Enrico Zapata? Oh, there's no one there by that name. I see. Are you by chance related to a Mr. Enrico Zapata? No? Well, you see, I found his wallet and it seems to have a sum of money in it. It looks as if he dropped it in something, tar perhaps. I can read the name, but the address and phone number have been obliterated. No, huh? Okay, well, thank you for your time."

"Why the story?" Tasha asked.

Jace shrugged. "We live in a cynical age, Tash. Some people get suspicious when complete strangers call them and ask for the phone numbers of their relatives or friends. This way they have a little incentive to open up to me."

Only once, with the last Zapata, did he deviate from his script. This Zapata at first claimed to know no Enricos, but changed his mind when Jace mentioned the wallet. "Oh, he's your brother, is he?" Jace said. "I see. And he lives with you. But I thought you said . . . Oh, I see. Well, I'll give you my phone number and if he can call and tell me how much money was in the wallet and what the wallet looks like, I'll be happy to return it to him." He gave a phone number and then repeated it.

"That's not your phone number," Tasha said when he hung up.

"As a matter of fact, it's the phone number of the public library," Jace said. "Not that it matters. He's never going to call back."

"You don't think he was telling the truth about knowing Enrico?"

"Not even close."

Tasha slumped back against the wall. "So much for that idea."

"I have one more call to make."

"You said there were seven Zapatas."

"Plus the pizza place." He was dialling before Tasha could protest. "Hello, Zapata Pizza? May I speak with Enrico Zapata, please?" There was a pause, then Jace's eyebrows shot up.

"What?" Tasha asked, leaning forward. "What?"

Jace opened his mouth to speak, then suddenly stiffened and shifted his attention back to the voice on the line. "Hello? Hello? Yes? Yes, that's right. I'm looking for the Enrico Zapata who used to be a waiter at the Fireside Café. Oh." He didn't look happy. "Yes, I see."

Tasha held her breath, crossed her fingers, and watched Jace's face for clues.

"Yes," Jace said sombrely. "Yes, okay. I see. Well, thank you."

Tasha could hardly believe her eyes when Jace hung up. The clunk of the receiver as it settled into the cradle sounded as final as the thud of a door slamming.

"Well," Jace said slowly, almost reluctantly. "I guess that just goes to show . . . that I'm the luckiest guy on earth!"

Tasha stared at him. What was he talking about?

"Come on," he said, jumping to his feet and burrowing in his pocket. Out came his car keys. "Let's go." He reached for her hand and pulled her up.

"Go where?"

"Zapata's Pizza and Wings. To talk to Enrico Zapata, former waiter at the Fireside Café."

"That was him?" Tasha couldn't believe her luck. "That was really him?"

"Actually, that was his nephew. Enrico is there, but he couldn't come to the phone," Jace said. "So what do you say we go over there and have a chat with him?"

* * *

Zapata's Pizza and Wings was the first pizza place Tasha had ever seen with a Tex-Mex decor. Cactus

74

and desert scenes were painted on the adobe style walls, and sombreros and serapes hung around the windows and on the dividers between booths.

"What'll it be?" a dark-haired young man asked when Tasha and Jace approached the counter.

Tasha looked around and spotted a familiar face over the divider between the dining area and the kitchen. "That's him," she said to Jace. "That's Enrico Zapata."

At that moment Enrico Zapata turned and glanced into the dining area. His eyes met Tasha's and he frowned. He came forward a few steps and peered at her again. Then, as if someone had thrown a switch, his entire face brightened. He burst out of the kitchen and came toward her. "You're Catherine Scanlan's daughter, aren't you?" he said.

Tasha nodded.

"I knew it!" Enrico Zapata grinned, pleased with himself. "You have the same eyes, the same mouth as your mother." Then his face went slack; his elation faded to sadness. "I heard what happened. A terrible thing. And today, very strange, someone called my nephew on the phone and asked if I used to work at the Fireside Café."

"That was me," Jace murmured.

"Ah." Enrico Zapata looked at Tasha again. "Come and sit down," he said.

They followed him to a table and waited while he insisted on ordering them his famous Zapata's Wild Cactus pizza. While they waited for it to appear Tasha took a deep breath and explained why she and Jace had come.

"The police have arrested my father for murder," she began. "But I don't believe he did it. I don't think he could ever do such a thing."

Enrico Zapata said nothing, which discouraged Tasha. Just for once she'd like someone to agree with her without hesitation. *Of course your father would never do such a thing, Tasha. Your father isn't that kind of man.*

"Mr. Zapata — "

"Please, call me Rico," he said. "Everyone does."

Tasha nodded. "Rico." The name felt funny in her mouth. "My mother walked out of our house very late on the night of August second," she said. "We never saw her again. All we know is that somehow she ended up at the Fireside Café. I was wondering, were you working that night? It was the night of the big storm, remember? The worst storm to hit the city since the 1920s."

As she paused, the waiter appeared with a pizza and a pitcher of cola.

"I remember that night," Enrico said, serving them each a slice of pizza. "I was at the Café, but I left early. I got a phone call from my cousin — I was living with him at the time. The wind was so bad that night that it lifted half the shingles off his roof. Rain was pouring in. What a terrible night." He paused and smiled at them both. "How do you like my pizza? Different, eh?"

Tasha had to admit that it was. It was the spiciest pizza she'd ever tasted.

"I don't use ordinary tomato sauce on it," Enrico said. "I use salsa. Plenty of hot, spicy salsa."

"Very interesting," Jace agreed. He washed

down each bite with several gulps of cola. "Now, about the night of the storm . . . "

"My poor cousin was going crazy on account of all the rain pouring into his house," Enrico said. "So I asked the manager — you remember him, Tasha. Mr. Horseballer."

"Close." Jace stifled a grin.

"I asked him, please can I go early, you know, so that I could help my cousin. And he said, sure. Business was pretty slow that night. So I went."

"Do you have any idea what time you left the restaurant?" Tasha asked.

Enrico shook his head. "It was a long time ago. I'd say eight-thirty. Maybe nine. I'm not sure."

Too early, Tasha thought. Her parents hadn't even been fighting at nine o'clock.

"But Mr. Horstbueller was at the Café when you left?" Jace asked. "Do you have any idea how long he stayed?"

Enrico shrugged. "Knowing him, he stayed until closing time. He was a guy who didn't like to take a chance he'd miss a customer. The place was supposed to be open eleven to one every day, and he made sure it was. He used to say, 'What happens if we close early and a customer shows up? That's a customer who'll never come back again. That's a customer who'll tell all his friends the Fireside Café doesn't keep its word.' I bet he was there the whole night."

Tasha and Jace exchanged glances. Enrico Zapata hadn't been at the restaurant late that night, so he hadn't seen Tasha's mother. But maybe there was still something he could help them with.

77

"I don't suppose you have any idea where we could find Mr. Horstbueller, do you, Enrico?" Tasha asked.

"Sure," Enrico said. He didn't hesitate even a moment. "I know exactly where you can find him. You know Mount Pleasant Road? Up around Lawrence Avenue?"

Tasha's heart raced. Finally, someone who would be able to tell her something.

"He lives up there?" Jace asked.

"He's buried up there. He's dead. Died five years ago, not long after the big storm."

Chapter Seven

Tasha looked in despair at Enrico Zapata.

"Dead?" she echoed. Locating Evart Horstbueller had been her best chance to find out when her mother had arrived at the Café, who she had arrived with or met there, and what might have happened after that. "Are you sure?" It was an idiotic question, she knew — how could you not be sure that someone was dead — but it slipped out before she could stop it.

"Am I sure?" Enrico said. "I went to the funeral. He died in an accident. A car accident, I think. At least, that's what they say."

"What do you mean?" Jace asked. "Are you saying it *wasn't* an accident?"

Enrico shrugged. "Things hadn't been going so well at the Café," he said. "The clientele had changed. The whole neighbourhood had changed. Instead of a nice neighbourhood with nice families, there was nothing but trouble. Every day there was something bad in the news, you know what I mean?"

Jace nodded. "Drugs and prostitution," he said. "And gangs."

"Exactly." Enrico shook his head sadly. "I hear it's improved a little since then, but for a few years it was bad. Really bad. A rough crowd started hanging around the Café. They scared away most of the old customers. Mr. Horseballer used to call the police two, maybe three times a day, but it never did any good. They always told him the same thing. Call us when someone commits a crime, they said. There's no law against a person going into a restaurant and ordering a cup of coffee or a piece of pie. So the business went downhill. I guess that's why your father decided to sell his interest in the place, huh?"

Tasha nodded, even though she wasn't paying much attention. She was so stunned to hear that Mr. Horstbueller had passed away that she couldn't concentrate on anything else.

"So who knows," Enrico went on. "A man is depressed. He works hard in life to build something and it falls apart. When a man has a car accident under such circumstances, who's to say it's really an accident?"

Tasha was trying to find another way around this latest news. Okay, so Mr. Horstbueller was dead. There had to be some other way, someone else who might know something. "What about the rest of the restaurant staff?" she asked. "Was there anyone else in the Café when you left that night to help your cousin?"

Enrico scratched his head and thought a moment. "Artie Jacobs was there, I guess. You remember him? He was the sous-chef."

"Do you know where we can find him?"

"Artie? He retired after the place was sold. Last I heard, he was somewhere in Florida. Fort Lauderdale? Maybe Tampa. Or maybe it was Arizona, one of those retirement places."

Another blow. She wasn't going to get anywhere, Tasha realized. As much as she wanted to, she wasn't going to be able to help her father.

"What about customers?" Jace asked. "Were there any regulars there? Anyone who might have known Tasha's mother?" From the tone of his voice Tasha knew that he was getting discouraged too.

"No one special," Enrico said. "Local hoods. A junkie or two. Nobody reliable, that's for sure." He looked at Tasha. "Sorry. I wish there was something useful I could tell you. I always liked your folks, you know. They were really nice people. Even your dad, back when he was cooking. He was a real good guy, even if he did lose it now and again."

"Lose it?" Tasha asked.

"You know, his temper. He used to really let loose sometimes, specially if something went wrong in the kitchen. He'd start flashing that big butcher knife of his around, giving everyone an earful — "

He broke off suddenly, and his eyes darted away from Tasha's. "I'm sorry," he murmured. "I don't mean that I think your old man — "

"It's okay," Tasha said. A lie. It wasn't okay at all. What if the police decided to question people who used to work at the Café? What would they think if they heard Enrico Zapata talk about her father's temper? The crown attorney would almost certainly want to use him as a witness — for the prosecution.

"Thanks for your time," she said as she stood up. Jace immediately sprang to his feet. "I'm glad to see you've done well since Dad sold the Café," she said graciously. "This is a very nice place."

"And interesting food," Jace said with enthusiasm. "I don't think I've ever had Tex-Mex pizza before."

"It was my daughter's idea," Enrico said. "I learned everything I know about the food business by working in restaurants, first as a bus boy, then as a waiter. My daughter, she learned in school. Studied restaurant management. How about that, eh? Now they teach kids in the classroom what you used to have to learn by doing." He laughed.

Daughter. The word reverberated in Tasha's head. Of course. Maybe there was another angle, another person who might have seen something that night, someone Mr. Horstbueller might have talked to about anything unusual that had happened.

"Do you remember how Mr. Horstbueller used to live on the other side of town from the Café?" she asked Enrico. "Remember how he refused to go for his driver's licence? He used to say there were too many nuts on the road."

"Sure," Enrico said, grinning. "His daughter used to drive him every day. Pick him up every night, too. I remember that because I remember thinking, that's some daughter. Drives all the way across town twice a day, and all because her old man is too stubborn to get himself a licence. A kid like that is really something special."

"Do you know if she still lives in the city?" Tasha asked.

"There weren't any Horstbuellers in the phone book," Jace reminded her.

"I heard she got married about a year after her father died," Enrico said.

Tasha nodded. That would explain why she wasn't listed under Horstbueller. She must have taken her husband's name.

"Do you know who she married?" Tasha asked.

Enrico Zapata shook his head. "Some guy in the funeral business, I heard. Pretty creepy, eh? All that death and sadness. Someone told me his name once, but I never met the guy. If I meet someone, I hardly ever forget his name. But a guy I never met?" He shrugged. "I'm not much help to you, am I, Tasha? But then I guess you're scraping the bottom of the barrel coming to see me. Horseballer's dead. Artie Jacobs is someplace in the States. And if you're here, obviously Mr. Durant couldn't help you."

Tasha stared at him. "Mr. Durant? You mean Denny Durant?"

"Sure," Enrico Zapata said. "You talked to him already, right?"

Tasha wasn't sure she understood what he meant. "Are you saying that Denny Durant was at the Fireside Café the night of the storm?"

Now it was Enrico Zapata's turn to look surprised. "Sure he was. He was there every night. Didn't know the first thing about running a restaurant — the only dough he ever made was as a hockey player — but he sure did like to sit at that table in the back, acting like a big shot. He told everyone he was there protecting his investment."

"His investment?" Now Tasha was completely lost.

"He owned half the place," Enrico Zapata said. "Didn't you know?"

She shook her head. Denny Durant owned half of the Fireside Café, and no one had ever bothered to mention this fact to her? It didn't seem possible. "Are you sure?" she asked.

"Sure I'm sure. He made a point of telling everyone a couple of dozen times a day. When your mother sold her half of the place, your dad took Denny Durant on as a kind of silent partner, only Denny was never silent about it."

"And you're absolutely positive that Denny was at the Fireside Café that night?"

"Yeah."

"Thank you Mr. — Thank you, Rico. Thanks a million."

"Don't tell me, let me guess," Jace said when they were outside. "You want to go to Lenny and Denny's."

Tasha nodded.

The Lenny and Denny's on Eglinton was the first of three her father had opened over the years. It was also the biggest, and the one where her father and Denny Durant maintained offices. Chances were good that they'd find Denny there.

"I must have passed this place a million times," Jace said, "but I've never been inside. It's got a real sports theme, doesn't it?" He gazed around at the

84

hockey photos, sweaters and other sports memorabilia that crowded the walls of the bar area to the right of the main door. A soccer game was playing on a big–screen television in one corner.

"The bar is the Denny's part of Lenny and Denny's," Tasha explained. "It's a sports bar. Denny runs it. The restaurant there — " she pointed to the entrance to the large dining room across from the bar " — is strictly family. Dad likes to say you can take the wife and kids there, and everybody will find something on the menu they'll like, at an affordable price."

She led him into the bar, where she approached the counter and asked the bartender if Mr. Durant was around.

"I'll check," he said, and headed for Denny Durant's office at the back of the bar. While they waited for him to return, Jace peered at some of the photos on the wall.

"Hey, those are real old-timers," he said. "*Famous* old-timers." He sounded impressed. "Look, that's Claude Dufresne. And there's Rick Morrow. Those guys were *big* stars in their time."

"So was Denny," Tasha said. "According to Denny." She barely glanced at the photos. She'd never been interested in professional sports, and particularly disliked hockey. The games always seemed to end in fist fights. Players were hauled off the ice, their faces swollen or their eyes bleeding, and the fans seemed to love it. It was no surprise, she thought, that so many of the players grinning out of the photos were missing at least one tooth, and that a bunch of others had scars on their faces.

She turned away in disgust just in time to see the bartender coming back toward them.

"You're going to have a wait a minute," he said. "He's got someone with him."

Just at that moment the door to the back office opened and a grim-faced man started out. He paused at the door and looked back inside. "I mean it, Denny," he growled. "You take care of this or you'll be sorry." The man stomped right past Jake and Tasha.

"I guess you can go on in," the bartender said.

"Who was that?" Jace whispered as they headed for Denny's office.

"Who knows?" Tasha said. "Denny rubs a lot of people the wrong way. Or maybe it was someone he owes money to. My dad says Denny gambles more than is good for him."

The door to the office was still open. Denny was straightening his tie. He flashed Tasha a smile and waved her in. "How ya doin', kid?" He pulled up a chair for her while he checked out Jace. "How are you holding up?"

"Okay, I guess," Tasha said. She introduced Jace and sat down.

"What a tough break," Denny said. "Tough all round, if you ask me. I guess it finally got to old Len, huh? He was so crazy about your mother. I used to tell him, you've got to relax, pal. You've got to give her some space. But he just couldn't do it. I guess the last straw was when she went back to school. He didn't handle that too well, if you know what I mean. And you know how he is when that temper of his blows. I mean, if you're smart, you'll stand back as far as you can get, am I right?" He shook his head, as if in awe of some fantastic picture playing in his mind. "I'm real sorry how all of this has turned out, kid."

Tasha had never liked Denny Durant. Her father and Denny had grown up together. Tasha suspected that her father had a blind spot when it came to Denny. But she didn't. She recognized Denny for what he was. He was too loud. He was too hungry for the prestige that came with owning Lenny and Denny's. He didn't even know much about the business. As far as she could tell, he sat in his office dreaming up crazy promotional schemes for the restaurants while her father did all the real work. And he insisted in calling Tasha "kid." She couldn't remember when he'd ever addressed her by name. Sometimes she wondered if he even knew what it was.

"It sounds like you think my father did it," she said, her voice as brittle as ice.

Denny blinked in surprise. His cheeks reddened. "Isn't that what the cops are saying? I mean, look, kid — "

"Tasha," she said. "My name is Tasha."

"Sure, I know that," Denny said, smiling at her. "Little Tasha–Taters. Isn't that what your mother used to call you?"

Tasha refused to return his smile. "Do you believe my father is innocent or don't you?"

"Look, Tasha," Denny said, "I can see you're upset. It's always a shock to find out things you don't want to know about people you love. But like I told the cops — "

"You talked to the police?" Tasha leapt to her feet.

"Sure, you could put it that way. I talked to them. They talked to me. They came here and asked me a bunch of questions, you know, on account of me being partners with your old man."

"What did you tell them?" Tasha asked.

"There wasn't much I *could* tell them," Denny said. The leather upholstery of his chair creaked as he shifted his weight. "Just that your folks had their problems. Sheesh, what married couple doesn't have problems? It's the reason I've never taken that walk down the aisle, you know what I mean?"

Tasha stared stonily at him.

"Anyway," Denny said, "so what if your dad used to explode every now and again? That doesn't necessarily prove anything, does it?" He laughed nervously. "Sure, he used to blow his top. He used to yell threats at her that people could hear ten blocks away. But, hey, that doesn't make the guy guilty, does it?"

Tasha stared at Denny Durant, whose small black eyes kept skipping away from her own. If he'd told the police what he'd just told her — and he had, he'd said he had — then he'd as good as announced to everyone that her father was guilty.

She'd never liked Denny Durant, but right now she hated him. At that moment, she began to understand how people's rage led them to do crazy things, things they might regret. Her hands curled into fists at her sides. She had to struggle with herself to keep from screaming at him. Her voice trembled as she spoke. "Were you are at the Fireside Café the night my mother disappeared?" she asked.

"Yeah," Denny said. "I was there for a while. Like I told the cops, I was there until about nine-thirty. Then, on account of the storm, and on account of business being so slow, I left."

Denny's voice grated on Tasha's nerves. He was speaking defiantly now, like a man who had done his civic duty instead of one who'd driven a knife into his partner's back. She asked him, "Did you see my mother that night?"

Denny Durant looked her straight in the eye. "No," he said. "I didn't."

"Who else was in the Café when you left?"

Denny's eyes began to smoulder like hot coals. "Look, kid, I understand you're upset. But you're not the cops. I don't have to sit here while you grill me like a steak, especially when you're doing it in that snotty tone of voice. I think I've had it with answering questions. Between the cops and the press, my phone has hardly stopped ringing. Plus all the business questions I'm handling while your old man's away. And now you."

Tasha stood her ground, despite her quivering knees. If she didn't control her anger, she wouldn't get any information out of him. She didn't like him, but she needed to know what he knew, whatever it was. "I — I'm sorry," she said. The words were bitter in her mouth. "I know you'd never do anything to hurt my father. Whatever you told the police, I'm sure it was what you saw and what you know. But just so you understand, I don't believe for a minute that my father did it."

"*We* don't think he did it," Jace said. Tasha

glanced at him, and saw in his eyes the same distaste for Denny Durant that she felt.

"I'm going to figure out for myself what happened. We talked to Enrico Zapata — "

Denny looked surprised. "Rico, huh? He still around?"

Tasha nodded. "He says you were in the Café when he left. So was Artie Jacobs."

"I hear Artie's down in the States somewhere. Or was. Maybe he kicked the bucket by now, huh?"

Tasha ignored the callous remark. "And Evart Horstbueller —"

"Definitely kicked the bucket, poor slob," Denny said.

"Do you have any idea who else was in the Café that night, or who was there when you left?"

The leather of Denny's chair crackled again as he leaned back and stared up at the ceiling a moment.

"No one else comes to mind, kid . . . er, Tasha. Like I said, I left early. I told old Evart to close up shop, but he was a stubborn one, that guy. He wouldn't lock up until closing time no matter what. They could declare World War Three and old Evart would keep those doors open." He shrugged. "You ever consider you might be barking up the wrong tree, kid?"

"What do you mean?"

"Well, if I follow your line of questioning, you're thinking that if your mother went to the Café, someone there must have seen her. Correct?"

Tasha nodded.

"Well, it ain't necessarily so. She had her own

keys to the place, you know. She could have gone there at any time of the day or night. She could have let herself in at three in the morning, for all anyone knows."

All the air drained out of Tasha. She felt faint and nauseous, all at the same time. What he'd said was true. She'd been following one line of reasoning. She hadn't considered there might be another, that perhaps her quest had been doomed from the start.

"Sorry, kid," Denny said. "I guess that isn't what you want to hear, huh?"

Tasha turned and stumbled toward the door. Then she felt something. Jace had taken hold of her elbow. He held on while he said, "Just one more thing, Mr. Durant. Mr. Horstbueller had a daughter. Do you happen to know where we could find her, or what her married name is?"

Denny frowned. "Why are you looking for her? She wasn't there."

"She picked her father up every night," Jace said. "We thought if anything unusual happened that night, he might have said something to her."

Denny shrugged. "Well, you got me, kid. I never even met the girl. I sure wasn't invited to the wedding, either. Sorry."

"Yeah," Jace murmured, as if he doubted regret could be found anywhere close to Denny Durant. "Sure."

Tasha and Jace left Denny's office and made their way to a table to go over their options. While Jace slurped a Coke Tasha tried to decide what she should do next. What *could* she do? Enrico Zapata couldn't help her. Neither could Denny. And Evart Horstbueller was dead. She stirred her straw around and around in her Coke, and wished her parents had been happier together so that none of this would be happening.

"Maybe there's some way we can trace the daughter," Jace said eventually.

"Maybe," Tasha said, although she had no idea how they'd go about doing that or whether it was even worth the effort. What if Denny was right? What if her mother had gone to the Café long after everyone had left? What if . . . "Jace, I know it's not exactly on the way home, but do you think we could drive by the Café?"

Jace nodded and beckoned a waiter for the bill. "No problem," he said. "Whatever you want."

"There's no charge for your drinks," the waiter said.

"No charge?"

"Mr. Durant says it's on the house." He nodded toward the back of the room where Denny was sitting at a table. He waved to them.

Without answering Denny's wave, Tasha got up and swept out of the room.

* * *

Five years is a long time to be away from a place, Tasha realized, as they drove along the streets only blocks from where the Café used to stand. The neighbourhood wasn't at all the same as she remembered it. The houses looked shabbier. Many of them needed new coats of paint, new windows. Some were fortunate enough to have occupants who cared about whether their tiny front lawns were mowed or not, but most were fronted by weed patches growing wildly on either side of cracked and crooked cement walkways.

The storefronts in the area were as dismal as the houses. Tasha remembered grocery stores and bakeries, and several little restaurants that drew enough diners to keep busy and to give the sidewalks a merry feel during long spring and summer evenings. Now there were as many stores with papered–over windows as there were thriving businesses, and thriving, Tasha realized, might have been overstating the case. The only places that seemed to be attracting much business were two dollar stores — the Loony Bin and Dollar Madness. The hardware store had a huge crack running diagonally through its plate-glass window. This had been half-heartedly taped up. No customers were visible through the dreary window of a little shoe store. And the place where the Fireside Café had been was now a huge hole in the ground, circled by a wooden fence, its entrance criss-crossed with bright yellow police tape. The awful realization struck her, once again, that her mother's body had lain here all these years.

She swallowed hard to keep her tears at bay and her emotions under control. "I guess there's no point in hanging around," she said, her voice trembling. She was sorry she'd come. If she stayed here a moment longer, that one sight, that horrible void, would replace all the sweet memories she had carried with her for so long. "Let's go."

No sooner had Jace flicked on his turn signal than Tasha called out, "No, wait! Stop the car!"

Jace slammed on the brakes. Tires squealed

behind them. Tasha whirled around just in time to see a black T-bird come within a fraction of rear-ending Jace's car. The driver looked angry.

"He's probably going to get out and hammer me," Jace said.

Instead, the driver of the T-bird pulled heavily on his steering wheel and sped past them.

Jace breathed a sigh of relief. "You okay?" he asked Tasha.

But Tasha was already jumping out of the car. "That woman," she shouted over her shoulder. "I have to catch up with that woman."

Chapter Eight

Tasha darted across the street, dodging cars whose startled drivers leaned on their horns. She didn't care. All her attention was focussed on the elderly woman wending her way down the street. Tasha didn't want to lose sight of her.

"Mrs. Mercer!" she called. "Mrs. Mercer!"

The old woman didn't turn. Maybe it isn't her, Tasha thought. Maybe my eyes, or my memory, have played a trick on me. But she didn't stop running until she reached the woman. Then she touched her shoulder. "Mrs. Mercer?"

The old woman jumped. When she turned to face Tasha, her hand was clamped over her heart and her eyes were wide with fear.

"Mrs. Mercer, I'm Natasha Scanlan. Remember me? My parents used to own the Fireside Café." She nodded towards the huge hole in the ground across the street. "Remember, Mrs. Mercer? You used to come over every Thursday afternoon for tea and scones. I used to bring them to you, with a little pot of my mother's homemade strawberry jam."

The old woman blinked. Slowly the fog of apprehension lifted from her face, until at last she looked merely puzzled. She peered at Tasha, and shook her head.

"I was smaller then," Tasha said quickly. "I was little."

Still the old woman said nothing, but continued to peer at Tasha through eyes that were sharp and bright. Then, very slowly, she began to nod. "Little Tasha Scanlan," she said.

Tasha smiled. "That's right. That's me."

Just then Jace came pounding up the sidewalk toward them, startling Mrs. Mercer, who clamped her hand over her heart again.

"It's okay," Tasha said. "This is my friend, Jason." She turned to Jace to explain. "Mrs. Mercer used to live right across the street from the Café. She came in for tea and scones once a week."

"Still do," Mrs. Mercer said.

For a moment, Tasha thought Mrs. Mercer was referring to her weekly visits to the Café. She was wondering how to delicately remind the old woman that the Café had been torn down, when it suddenly occurred to her that Mrs. Mercer wasn't talking about scones and homemade strawberry jam. "You mean you still live in the same apartment?" she asked. "On top of the shoe store?"

Mrs. Mercer nodded. "Except it isn't a shoe store any more. It's a dollar store."

"Mrs. Mercer, I was wondering — "

"Would you and your friend like to come up for

96

tea?" the old lady asked. "I've been out doing some errands and my feet are sore." She shook her head. "I used to be able to tromp through the woods all day and never feel a thing. Not any more, though. I was just on my way home to put on the kettle. Come and join me."

Tasha looked at Jace, who shrugged. "I've got an hour on the meter."

"We'd love to," Tasha said. It would give her a chance to ask Mrs. Mercer what she remembered about the night of the storm, and whether anyone else who'd lived in the area five years ago was still around.

Although Mrs. Mercer had been a regular at the Fireside Café, and lived directly across from it, Tasha had never been inside her apartment. As she and Jace followed the old woman up a dimly lit flight of stairs and into an equally gloomy hallway, off which were doors to four apartments, Tasha held her breath. With such an unpromising entrance, she was afraid that Mrs. Mercer's place would turn out to be dreary and depressing. Her fears were rein-forced when the door directly across from them popped open and a greying head peeked out, stared at her and Jace and Mrs. Mercer, and then disap-peared back inside. The door closed with a click.

"That woman drives me crazy," Mrs. Mercer said. "She's so nosey. One of these days she's going to get herself arrested."

"For being nosey?" Jace asked. He sounded baffled.

"For bothering the police all the time," Mrs. Mercer said. "For reporting suspicious goings-on.

Mr. Turner at the end of the hall there didn't come home for two days. She — " She nodded at her neighbour's door. " — reported him missing to the police."

"Wasn't he missing?" Jace asked.

Mrs. Mercer shook her head. "He'd met a woman. He stayed over at her place for the weekend. And he was not at all amused to come home to find the police waiting at his door, expecting him to account for his whereabouts."

As Mrs. Mercer unlocked the door to her apartment Tasha glanced at Jace, who shook his head as if to confirm what she was feeling: strange place, strange people.

Mrs. Mercer's apartment was not at all what Tasha had expected. As soon as she and Jace stepped inside, they were drenched in bright sunlight from the enormous picture window in the living room. The entire flat was painted in sunny yellows and eggshell blues, and its walls were hung with brilliantly coloured paintings and photos — almost all of them depicting birds. Some were exotic species — parrots, cockatoos, flamingos — while others, more muted in colour but still beautiful, were North American. Tasha recognized Canada geese in flight, bluejays, cardinals, snowy owls, ptarmigans. But there were as many types that she couldn't name.

"You have quite a collection here," Jace said, staring around, his mouth gaping a little as he looked from painting to photo to sketch, all beautifully framed.

Mrs. Mercer seemed pleased by his reaction.

"I've been a bird lover all my life," she said. "The paintings are all purchases — I couldn't draw a straight line if my life depended on it. But the photographs are my own work." She smiled. "I'm a bit of . . . well . . . of an amateur photographer."

Tasha looked again at the photos. Some were in colour, others, often more dramatic in composition, were black and white.

"Please look around," Mrs. Mercer said. "I'll just go and make the tea. I won't be a minute." She disappeared into the kitchen.

Tasha and Jace circled the living room, taking a closer look at the spectacular photography. To each frame a little metal plate had been attached bearing the name of the bird and the date the photo had been taken.

"She must have travelled all over North America to get these," Tasha said. "Look at these rock ptarmigans. They're native to the Arctic." She paused then at the picture window and looked down into the street. From where she stood, she had a clear view of the hole in the ground where the Café used to stand. To one side of the window, facing it, was a big cosy armchair and a table, stacked with books, on which sat a reading lamp. Perched on one of the heap of books was a pair of half-glasses — reading glasses, Tasha realized. She imagined Mrs. Mercer sitting there, a book in her lap, glancing up every now and then to see what was happening in the street below. It was possible, very possible, that she had seen something the night that Tasha's mother had disappeared.

"Hey, check this out," Jace said.

Tasha crossed the room to look at a colour photo of two cardinals, a male with his bright red jacket sitting beside the female, her colours a softer reddish brown rather than scarlet. She was leaning in to the male, on a fence in what looked like an alleyway. Tasha could see brimming trash cans and garbage bags in the background.

"Such beautiful birds in such an ugly urban setting," Jace said. "What a great picture."

"I had no idea," Tasha murmured. Most of the photos were as good as anything she had seen in *National Geographic*. "To me, she was just this little old lady who dressed funny and loved tea and scones. She used to come in wearing a long tweedy sort of skirt, an old bush jacket, and a pair of what looked like combat boots. She always had a backpack slung over one shoulder. I guess she'd been out birding and was stopping off for a cup of tea before going home." She shook her head in admiration. "It's funny how you get an impression of people that turns out to be totally wrong. I always thought she was borderline crazy. It turns out she's really talented."

"Here we are!" said Mrs. Mercer. Tasha whirled around, her cheeks burning. She hoped the old woman hadn't overhead her. Mrs. Mercer was carrying a tray laden with a teapot, cups, sugar, milk and a plate of cake. "Please, sit down," she said. "I'll pour."

Tasha accepted a cup of tea and a slice of cake, which she devoured. She hadn't realized how hungry she was. While Mrs. Mercer put another piece of cake on her plate, Tasha broached the subject of her mother.

100

"Oh, yes," Mrs. Mercer said, her voice crackling with distress, "I did hear about that. What a terrible thing!"

"That's why I'm glad I ran into you, Mrs. Mercer. I wanted to ask you a few questions."

"Questions?" Mrs. Mercer's cup rattled against its saucer. "What kind of questions?"

Tasha outlined the facts surrounding her father's arrest, and explained that she and Jace were doing their best to find out what had really happened that night.

"Oh dear," Mrs. Mercer said. Her hands trembled as she set the teacup on the table. "Oh dear."

"We've been trying to locate people who might have seen anything at the Café that night, anything at all. We tried to locate Mr. Horstbueller — you remember him, he managed the Café for my parents. But he died in an accident a few years ago. And now we've run into you. You must remember that night. It was the big storm. Trees came down all over town. I was wondering, Mrs. Mercer, did you happen to look out the window that night? Did you happen to see my mother arrive at the Café?"

"Oh!" Mrs. Mercer cried, as if she had been sharply poked. "Oh my, no."

Tasha exchanged glances with Jace. The question clearly distressed the old woman. But why? "Please, Mrs. Mercer, it's really important. Can you remember anything about that night?"

"The neighbourhood has changed so much," Mrs. Mercer said. "There were always unsavoury people hanging around." She gave a little shudder at the thought.

"But did you see anything? Anything at all?" Tasha said eagerly. Perhaps too eagerly. The old woman looked even more alarmed.

"As far as we can see," Jace said, his tone more relaxed, more soothing than Tasha's, "the police are concentrating on proving that Tasha's father is guilty. They don't seem to be considering any other suspects. We thought if we could come up with some new information — any kind of new information — they might take another look at the case. So if you happened to see Mrs. Scanlan arrive at the Café that night, and if she happened to be with anyone other than Mr. Scanlan, or if you recognized anyone you saw going into or coming out of the Café that night, it could really help us. You understand, don't you, Mrs. Mercer?"

"Yes," the old woman said slowly. "I understand, but I'm afraid I can't help you."

"You weren't home that night?"

"Oh, I was home," she said. "You'd have to be crazy to go out on a night like that." She glanced apologetically at Tasha. "I mean, at my age you'd have to be crazy. I was right here, curled up in my chair, reading."

"The chair over there?" Tasha said, gesturing toward the comfortable armchair in front of the big plate-glass window.

"I — I suppose so," Mrs. Mercer said. "Yes, I suppose it must have been there. But I'm afraid I didn't see anything." She laughed, and sounded uncomfortable. "My eyesight isn't what it used to be," she said. "Even if I had been peering out that window, which, I assure you, I was not, I wouldn't have been able to see much. I'm old. When you're old, things don't work as well as they used to. I'm afraid my eyesight isn't what it used to be. I'm sorry, dear."

"That's okay," Tasha said. Another bitter disappointment. Why couldn't she be lucky just for once? Why couldn't Mrs. Mercer say something like, *"Why, now that you mention it, I did see her arrive. And there was this man with her. No, it wasn't your father. It was another man. A man with a black moustache . . ."* Tasha would happily have given anything she had and anything she was ever likely to get in life just to hear the words that would set her father free. But it didn't appear that was going to happen today.

"Is there anyone else in the neighbourhood who might be able to help us, Mrs. Mercer?" Jace asked. "Anyone who was living here five years ago who might have seen something that night?"

Mrs. Mercer thought a moment and then shook her head. "I'm sorry," she said. "I can't think of anyone."

Tasha and Jace thanked the old woman for her time. Tasha had to force herself to sound gracious as she said goodbye at the door of the apartment. As she and Jace turned toward the stairs, the door on the other side of the hallway opened and the same wrinkled old face peeked out. The door closed again as quickly as it had opened. Tasha trudged down the stairs into the bright sunshine. There didn't seem to be anything she could do to help her father.

"Sorry, Tash," Jace said when he dropped her off at her house. "I know you were hoping we'd turn up something. Maybe tomorrow we'll get lucky, huh?"

"Sure," Tasha said, although she didn't believe it for a minute. What could possibly turn up? She didn't even know where to start looking. She was completely out of ideas. But Jace was trying hard to be optimistic, and she didn't want to make him feel worse. "Sure, I'll talk to you tomorrow."

Aunt Cynthia was sitting in the living room, and jumped to her feet the moment Tasha walked through the door.

"Where have you been?" she said. "You've been gone all day. You didn't even call. I had no idea where you were."

Tasha was caught off guard. Aunt Cynthia sounded more worried than angry, the same as Tasha's father would have been if he were home and she had taken off without telling him where she had gone. Maybe Aunt Cynthia didn't think very highly of Leonard Scanlan, and maybe she'd had her differences with Catherine Scanlan, but she seemed to be taking her responsibility for Tasha seriously. "I'm sorry," Tasha said. "I should at least have called. It won't happen again."

"Where were you?" Aunt Cynthia's voice was softer now.

"Here and there."

"Trying to help your father, I suppose."

Tasha stiffened. "That's right," she said, bracing for an argument.

Aunt Cynthia sighed and sank down onto the sofa. She shook her head slowly. "We didn't get off to a very good start yesterday, did we?" she said.

"And you've been out all day today, so we haven't had a chance to talk. Sit down, Tasha."

Tasha remained standing.

"Please?" Aunt Cynthia pleaded. "Like it or not, Tasha, we're going to be living under this roof together for a while. There's no one else to take care of you. Please sit down. There's something I have to say."

Grudgingly, Tasha dropped down onto the far end of the sofa. She was in no mood for another tirade against her parents.

"I don't have children," Aunt Cynthia began. "I've never even been married. People who know me well say that's because I shoot off my mouth first and ask questions later." She started to laugh, but stopped abruptly when Tasha didn't join her. "What I'm trying to say is, I'm sorry. I had no right to say what I said last night. It was completely insensitive of me to blast in here talking about *my* feelings and *my* ancient history. I should have paid more attention to how you were feeling about all of this. I know he's your father, Tasha. Maybe I haven't always seen eye to eye with him, and he hasn't always seen eye to eye with your mother, but when it comes right down to it, if I were in your shoes, I don't think I'd act any differently from the way you are now."

Tasha eyed her aunt for a moment before replying. Did this mean that Aunt Cynthia believed her father was innocent? She hadn't actually said that. Probably she believed what she'd said last night — that at the very least the police were right to have arrested him and to be treating him as their prime suspect. Tasha told herself she didn't care what Aunt Cynthia thought — nothing was going to change *her* mind. In the meantime, though, her aunt was right. They had to live together. Aunt Cynthia was responsible for her until her father came home. And if that turned out to be a very long time . . . Tasha shook the thought from her mind. She had to force herself to stay positive. There was nothing to be gained from feeling hopeless.

"It would mean a lot to me if you'd accept my apology," Aunt Cynthia said. "We could start all over again. Okay?" She thrust out her hand. It took Tasha a moment to realize that she was supposed to shake it.

"Okay," Tasha said.

Aunt Cynthia smiled at her. "Hungry?"

Tasha wasn't, but she knew that her aunt wanted her to be. She could smell something cooking. "Something smells good," she said. At least that was the truth.

Aunt Cynthia smiled. "Great. There's a batch of my world famous Italian sausage and vegetable soup simmering on the stove. And I have a fresh baguette and some cheese."

* * *

Tasha lay on her bed, fully dressed, and stared up at the darkened ceiling. Aunt Cynthia's soup was among the best she had ever tasted. It was as good as anything her father had ever made, but more interesting, more daring. It was thick with chunks of spicy sausage, sweet red and yellow peppers, and pungent with spices Aunt Cynthia had had to name for her.

"I call it my East Indian–South Asian home-made Italian soup," Aunt Cynthia had said, beaming under Tasha's compliments. "I'm famous for it back in Walla Walla."

Tasha had excused herself soon after clearing away the supper dishes, saying how tired she felt.

"No problem," Aunt Cynthia had replied, cheerier now that she felt she had cleared the air.

Tasha lay on her bed for hours, wondering how her father was, and whether she could see him. She decided she'd try first thing in the morning. She wondered, too, what else she could do to help him. Who else could she talk to? Who else might have been in or near the Fireside Café that night? Who else might have seen something?

Mrs. Mercer had said there was no one left in the neighbourhood who had lived there five years ago. Still, she could be wrong. It was possible that if Tasha and Jace went door-to-door they might turn up someone who had seen something, anything at all, that might help her father. She had to get him out of jail. She just had to.

Frustration formed like a knot in her stomach. Her father was innocent. He *had* to be innocent, because if he wasn't . . . She squeezed her eyes shut, as if that could drive doubt from her mind. Because if he wasn't innocent, that meant she had been living with a murderer for the past five years. It meant that the letters he'd produced, supposedly written by her mother, had been phoney, and that the sympathy he'd shown her whenever she felt miserable or when the ache in her heart from her mother's absence overwhelmed her, was phoney too. His supposed

107

reassurances might have been the ghoulish act of a cold-blooded murderer. If he'd done what they said, every word that had come out of his mouth whenever he comforted her had been calculated, and with each word he spoke, he'd known in his heart that the mother Tasha missed so desperately had been laid to her final terrible rest a long, long time ago.

It wasn't possible.

It simply wasn't possible.

If only Mrs. Mercer had seen something.

If only. Her father had once called them the two saddest words in the English language. Words of regret, of despair. Words of worlds that might have been, but never could be.

Tasha sat bolt upright. Of course! She should have seen it before. She should have put two and two together when she was in the old woman's apartment. Mrs. Mercer had seemed so upset by Tasha's questions. At the time Tasha had thought that it was the subject of the questions that had made her so nervous. Now she knew it was something else.

She swung her feet over the side of her bed and reached for the phone on her bedside table. Quickly she dialled Jace's number, and then held her breath while the phone rang. It was past eleven. Mr. and Mrs. Bhupal wouldn't appreciate such a late phone call.

"Please," she whispered into the dark. "Please let Jace be the one who answers."

"Hello?"

Yes! "Jace?"

"Tasha. What's up?"

"She was lying."

"What?"

"Mrs. Mercer. She was lying. Didn't you see the pictures in her apartment?"

"Well sure, but — "

"The pictures she *took*, I mean. The photographs. They had dates on them. Did you notice that?"

"Yes, but — "

"Some of them were taken almost exactly five years ago. Some were taken even later, two or three years ago."

"Tash," Jace said slowly, "you've lost me."

"Mrs. Mercer said she was sitting in her chair that night, the chair right in front of the picture window that overlooks the Café. She said she was sitting right there but that she didn't see anything because her eyes were so bad. Remember?"

"Yes . . . "

"If her eyes were so bad five years ago, how did she manage to take such spectacular photographs? She was still taking them a couple of years later."

"Maybe she wears glasses."

"She does, Jace. I saw them, sitting on a stack of books on that table next to her reading chair. But they were half-lens glasses. When people wear half-lenses like that I'm sure it's because they only need glasses for reading. I bet Mrs. Mercer sees distant things perfectly."

There was a long pause on the other end of the line. When Jace finally spoke again, he sounded almost as excited as she was. "So this means — "

"This means she also saw distances perfectly well five years ago. Which means she lied to us when she said she wouldn't have been able to see anything across the street. And didn't you notice how nervous she seemed all of a sudden when we started talking about that night? She lied to us, Jace. She's hiding something. Maybe she saw something five years ago that scared her. Something that's making her lie about it now, five years later."

She heard Jace's gentle breathing as he contemplated this piece of information.

"So," he said at last, "what do you want to do about it?"

"I think we should go back there tomorrow. I think we should confront her."

"I'll pick you up at ten," Jace said.

Tasha grinned. He said it just like that, like, of course she was right, of course they had to go back, no matter how the old woman might react to their showing up on her doorstep again, like it was the only option and she was perfectly right to suggest it. A wave of gratitude washed over her. She tried to imagine doing all of this on her own, without someone by her side who believed in her.

"Jace?"

"Yeah?"

"I really appreciate this, you know."

"What, going over there with you?"

"No," she said. "I mean everything. Believing in my dad, helping me out, everything."

"No problem," Jace said. "Isn't that what friends are for?"

* * *

Tasha was dressed and waiting at the curb when Jace pulled up in front of her house the next morning. As she buckled her seatbelt, he produced a small brown paper bag, which he thrust at her. "What is it?"

"One of Mom's homemade lemon and poppy-seed muffins," Jace said. "My mom has this idea you're probably not eating right. I promised her I'd stand over you with a big stick if I had to, to make sure you ate this."

Tasha opened the bag and sniffed the contents.

"I don't think you'll need that stick," she said, finishing off the muffin while they drove across town. This could be her father's big break. In another hour, she could well be on her way to the police station with the critical piece of evidence that would set her father free.

Tasha and Jace let themselves in the door next to the dollar store entrance. Tasha was so impatient that she took the stairs two at a time. She was rapping loudly on Mrs. Mercer's apartment door by the time Jace joined her. There was no answer.

"Maybe she went to church," Jace said. "It *is* Sunday."

Tasha slumped against the door. She hadn't thought of that. Just then a head poked out from one of the doors on the other side of the hall. It was the same head that had peeked out yesterday.

"Excuse me," Tasha said, "but do you know where Mrs. Mercer is?"

The woman looked alarmed and started to pull back.

"Wait!" Tasha called. "We're friends of Mrs. Mercer's. We were here yesterday, remember?"

The door opened wider, revealing a woman

111

wearing a baggy purple track suit. She appeared to be even older than Mrs. Mercer.

"I remember," she said, her voice thin and shaky with age.

"Do you happen to know where Mrs. Mercer is now?" Tasha asked. "It's very important that we speak to her."

"I don't think you'll be able to," the old woman said. "She's in the hospital."

"What?"

"They think it was an accident," the old woman said, "even though I told them it was no such thing. I told them there was nothing accidental about it. I told them, he was trying to kill her."

"Who was?" Tasha asked. "Who was trying to kill Mrs. Mercer?"

"Why, the man who pushed her down the stairs, of course," the old woman said. "You don't push a person down the stairs unless you want to hurt them, and you don't push them that hard unless you intend to kill them."

Chapter Nine

Tasha stared at the old woman. "You mean you actually *saw* someone push Mrs. Mercer down the stairs?"

"Yes," the woman said, nodding excitedly. "That's exactly what I mean. I told them when they came for her. I told them someone pushed her, someone was trying to kill her, but they didn't do anything about it."

"They?" Tasha asked.

"The ones that came in the ambulance. I told them, I said, Edith didn't jump down those stairs, you know. She was pushed by an evil man."

Jace arched an eyebrow and exchanged glances with Tasha. "Did you by any chance recognize the man, Mrs. . . . ?"

"Zadoor," the old woman said. "Mrs. Maimie Zadoor. Mr. Zadoor was a circus performer, you know. The Great Zadoor, they called him. He was an escape artist, better even than Houdini."

Jace smiled indulgently at her. "Mrs. Zadoor, did you actually see the man who pushed Mrs. Mercer down the stairs?"

"I did. He was tall," Mrs. Zadoor said. "Very tall. And he had yellow hair — "

"Blond, you mean?"

"I mean yellow," Mrs. Zadoor said. "As bright as a buttercup. And he had a bird on his face."

"A bird?" Jace looked sceptical.

"A bird," the old woman said. "On his cheek."

"You mean a tattoo?" Jace asked.

"Not a tattoo. A bird. Looked like a heron, if you ask me, although Edith may have a more precise idea. She's very fond of birds, you know."

"Yes," Tasha said. "I know. Did you recognize the man, Mrs. Zadoor? Have you ever seen him before?"

Mrs. Zadoor shook her greying head.

"Did you tell the ambulance attendants about the man with the bird on his face?" Jace asked.

"You bet I told them. I told them they should call the police, they should find the man and arrest him."

"And did they call the police?"

"Not that I saw." Mrs. Zadoor frowned. "They think I'm crazy. I was a fire-eater, did I tell you that? Swallowed swords, too. You have to be smart to do that, not crazy. I told them, find the man with the bird on his face, he's the one who pushed her. But they didn't do a thing. Just packed her in the back of the ambulance and took her away to the hospital."

"Do you happen to know which hospital?" Tasha asked.

"Western General," Mrs. Zadoor said.

They thanked the old woman and went back downstairs.

"She's a fire eater, and I'm a psychic," Jace said as he unlocked the car door. "I'm reading your mind even as I speak."

"Yeah? What do you see?"

"I see that you want to go to Western General Hospital."

"It's nice to know that if all that computer stuff doesn't work out for you," Tasha said, "you have something you can fall back on."

"Psychic reader, you mean?"

"Or chauffeur."

Half an hour later Tasha sat in the passenger seat of Jace's car, staring blankly ahead. She'd leapt out of bed in the morning filled with optimism. Today was going to be the day, she'd thought. Mrs. Mercer knew something and Tasha was going to get her to reveal it. Then she was going to use Mrs. Mercer's information to have her father set free. At least, that had been her plan. But it didn't look now as if things were going to work out the way she'd hoped. She and Jace had rushed over to the hospital only to have the nurse at the front desk tell them, "I'm afraid Mrs. Mercer isn't allowed any visitors."

"Not even for a minute?" Jace pleaded. "It's very important. Tasha is Mrs. Mercer's grand-daughter. They're very close."

Tasha had to struggle to hide her surprise, but it didn't do any good.

"I'm very sorry, dear," the nurse said, her voice sympathetic but firm. "Your grandmother is very sick. She's in a coma. The doctor has left strict orders — no visitors. Why don't you call later this afternoon? Maybe there'll be a change in her condition."

Coma. The word reverberated in Tasha's mind. Mrs. Mercer was old. If she was in a coma, there was a chance she might never come out of it. In that case, whatever she knew, whatever had made her lie about what had happened that night five years ago, would remain a secret forever.

Tasha glanced out of the car window now, and saw Jace approaching.

"Here we go," he said, his voice casual. Tasha knew, though, that he wasn't feeling as cheery as he pretended. He was forcing a good mood only for her benefit. "Two caffe latte and one almond croissant. Are you sure you don't want anything to eat?"

"Positive," Tasha said. She took both cups from him so he could slide in behind the steering wheel. They pried the lids off their coffees and sat quietly for a moment.

"So," Jace said after a few bites of his croissant. "What next? I was thinking maybe we could knock on doors in Mrs. Mercer's neighbourhood, you know, see if we can turn up anyone else who might remember seeing something."

"I thought of that, too," Tasha said.

"You don't sound very enthusiastic. Do you want to try something else? Do you want to go to the police? We could tell them what happened to Mrs. Mercer, and what Mrs. Zadoor said."

"You mean, that Mrs. Mercer was pushed down the stairs by a man with a bird on his face?"

"That's what happened, isn't it?"

"Maybe," Tasha agreed, "but, come on, Jace, it sounds pretty weird, doesn't it — a guy with yellow hair and a bird on his face? Besides, how do we know that the man who pushed her had anything to do with my mother? Maybe he pushed her for some other reason. Maybe there was some kind of feud going on in the birding world and Mrs. Mercer got herself caught up in it."

Jace gave her a wry look. "And you think *that* doesn't sound weird?"

Tasha sighed. She was fresh out of ideas. She drained the rest of the caffe latte from her cup and replaced the lid. "Okay," she said. "The cop shop it is. Maybe they'll let me see my dad."

"*And* you'll tell them about Mrs. Mercer and the birdman, right?" Jace said. "It couldn't hurt. And you never know, Tash. It might help."

Tasha sighed. "Sure," she said. "Why not?"

* * *

Why not? Why not tell the police about Mrs. Mercer and the birdman? Well, how about because they'd think she was crazy? You see, officer, this admittedly nutty old woman with a history of seeing suspicious activities where none exists saw a man with hair as yellow as a buttercup and a heron on his face . . . *sure* they'd believe that — about the same time that agreed that Earth was being overrun by little green men from Mars. Most likely they'd think she was a nuisance — a little girl playing at grown-up games. Or, worse, an obstructor of justice.

"Let me get this straight," Detective Pirelli said when Tasha finished recounting her story. "Some

117

old sword swallower tells you a neighbour of hers took a tumble down a flight of stairs and you think this has something to do with your father being in lock-up? Is that what you're trying to tell us?" The irritation in his voice was as sharp as a needle. He shook his head as he glanced across his desk at Detective Marchand.

Tasha's cheeks burned, partly because the story sounded so improbable when she looked at it mirrored in Detective Pirelli's eyes, and partly because his voice was so loud that a half-dozen other people in the squad room turned to look at her.

"Mrs. Zadoor says she saw the whole thing," Tasha said. "She says the man was tall — "

"Mrs. Zadoor is four-foot-ten," Detective Marchand said gently. "To her, anyone over five feet is tall."

Tasha frowned. How did Detective Marchand know Mrs. Zadoor's height? Come to think of it, how did Detective Pirelli know Mrs. Zadoor was a retired sword swallower? Tasha hadn't mentioned that. She'd been afraid those facts would only make her story sound even more improbable.

"You've already spoken to Mrs. Zadoor, haven't you?" Tasha said, more discouraged than ever. Talked to her and dismissed what she had to say, she added to herself.

"I don't think there's an officer in this division who *hasn't* spoken to her at one time or another," Detective Pirelli said. "The woman's a nuisance. One of these days I'm going to cite her for making a false report."

"The ambulance guys called us," Detective

Marchand explained. Her tone was kinder, less exasperated. "Because of what Mrs. Zadoor told them, and because of the location — right across from where the Fireside Café used to be — we looked into it. But to tell you the truth, Tasha, Mrs. Zadoor isn't credible. She has too much of a history around here. And nobody else seems to have seen anything."

"But Mrs. Mercer was pushed," Tasha insisted.

"Fell or pushed, who knows?" Detective Pirelli said. "Either way, there's nothing that ties this incident to your father."

"But Mrs. Mercer *lied* to me," Tasha said. "She said she didn't see anything that night, but she did."

"She didn't tell you that, Tasha," Detective Marchand said.

"But I *know* she was lying. You weren't there. You didn't see how agitated she got as soon as we asked her about that night. She lied about her poor eyesight too."

Detective Marchand fixed Tasha with her purple-flecked eyes. "There's not much we can do until we have a chance to talk to Mrs. Mercer and find out what really happened," she said. "But I promise you this, Tasha. The minute she wakes up, I'll go to the hospital and I'll speak with her. I'll also ask her about what she saw that night. Okay?"

Tasha looked at Detective Marchand's sympathetic face, then at Detective Pirelli's harder, colder one, and knew that this was the best she could hope for. "Okay," she said. Then, "Can I see my father?"

"Sure," Detective Marchand said. "He's in the remand centre, though."

"The what?"

"Remand. That's where they keep people until their cases come to trial. He's over at the Don Jail. You wait here. I'll arrange it, and take you over there."

* * *

Leonard Scanlan looked grey and haggard. The clothes he was wearing — jeans and a pale blue shirt, neither of them his own — hung on him like a sack draped over a beanpole. Tears welled up in Tasha's eyes as she peered at him through thick plexiglass. She ducked her head to wipe them away so he wouldn't see she was crying. Then she fumbled for the phone receiver so she could talk to him.

"I'm fine," he insisted. It pained Tasha to see the pitifully forced look of optimism in his eyes. "It's you I'm worried about. How are you getting along with Aunt Cynthia?"

"Okay, I guess."

"I hope it won't be too much longer," he said, smiling bravely. "I have a hearing tomorrow morning. Mr. Brubaker seems to think I have a chance of getting out on bail. He'll be coming to see you this evening. He wants you to be at the hearing. I told him I didn't think it was a good idea — besides, you have school. But he wants you there. He — " Her father hung his head, as if ashamed. "He thinks things might go better if the judge sees I'm a family man, and my daughter is there supporting me."

Tears sprang again to Tasha's eyes. She longed to reach right through the glass and hug her father, so he would know for sure that she loved him. "Of course I support you, Daddy. I know you didn't do it, and I'll do anything to help you. Anything at all." She held her hand flat against the glass. Her father looked up at her, his own eyes moist with tears, and he, too, held up a hand, and pressed it flat against hers.

Tasha's voice trembled as she said, "Dad? Can I ask you something?"

Her father nodded listlessly.

"That night," Tasha said. She hated to have to ask. Forming the words felt like an act of betrayal. "That night, after you and Mom had that big argument and you went out, where did you go?"

Her father's gaze slipped away from her. He stared down at the floor for what seemed an impossibly long time. When he looked back up, his eyes kept skittering away from her.

"I . . . I needed some air," he said. "I needed to think."

"But it was a storm, Dad. And you left me all alone in the house."

"I know," he said, his voice anguished. "I know, Tasha, and I'm sorry. I . . . I wasn't thinking clearly. I loved your mother. I thought she was leaving me for good. I had to get out of the house. I had to think."

The next question was even harder than the first, and she asked it in a voice that was barely a whisper.

"Where did you go?"

"For a drive," he said. "I don't even know where I went. I just drove around and around, and then I went home."

It wasn't the answer she'd been looking for. It was too vague. The crown attorney would say that he had no real alibi. Her father's evasiveness in answering didn't inspire much confidence either.

"What about the letters?" Tasha asked.

"Letters?"

"The letters from Mom. Didn't you think it was funny that they were typed? Mom hated to type. She wasn't even very good at it."

Her father looked blankly at her. His passivity infuriated Tasha.

"Didn't it occur to you that maybe Mom didn't write those letters? That maybe someone else did?"

He shook his head slowly, so slowly that Tasha wasn't even sure he was responding to what she had said. She decided it would be pointless to ask him her final question: Why did you destroy the letters? Why didn't you save them like you promised you would?

Too soon, her father had to leave. As Tasha watched him being led through a heavy metal door she gave up the struggle to control her tears.

* * *

"If I wanted to find out who someone married," Tasha asked Detective Marchand as they left the jail, "what would be the best way?"

Detective Marchand peered at her long and hard. "Are you okay, Tasha?"

Oh, sure, Tasha wanted to snap at her. My mom's dead, my dad's in jail, you're working around the clock to make sure he stays there — I'm perfectly fine, thank you very much. "I've had better days," she said instead. "Not to mention better weeks, and better months." She forced a smile, so that Detective Marchand would be more likely to answer her question. "So, suppose I used to know someone and that someone got married and changed her name, but I didn't know what she changed it to. How would I go about trying to find her?"

Detective Marchand's eyes narrowed and Tasha knew she was wondering if the question had anything to do with Tasha's father. But she didn't ask. Instead, she said, "Do you have any idea where this person was married? Here in the city? Or at least in this province?"

"I think it was here," Tasha said, although, now that she thought about it, it could have been anywhere.

"In that case, you can go down to the Registrar General," Detective Marchand said. "They keep all the information on marriages, births and deaths. They might be able to help you."

Tasha was surprised that the detective didn't press her for any further information. Tomorrow, when the government offices opened, she'd see what she could find out.

Chapter Ten

"Our objective tomorrow is to try to get your father out on bail," Mr. Brubaker said.

"*Try?*" Tasha repeated.

"He's charged with murder. It could be tough," the lawyer admitted. "But it's worth a try. We're going to have to work together on this. *My* job will be to argue that your father should be released pending his trial. *Your* job is to do what you can to give the judge confidence that your father is a loving, caring man whose family believes in him one hundred percent, and who poses no risk to society. Do you understand, Natasha?"

Tasha nodded at her father's lawyer, who was settled on the sofa with a mug of Aunt Cynthia's coffee on the table in front of him. He had marched into the house as if he were an old friend and, before he started talking about Leonard Scanlan's court hearing, had taken a few minutes to assure Tasha that there was every reason to be optimistic about her father's case. She wanted desperately to believe him, but when she asked how he planned to counter the charges made by the police, he merely smiled and said, "Suppose you let me worry about that." Then, before Tasha could press him further, he turned to Aunt Cynthia and said, "Any chance of a cup of coffee?" When she brought him some, he'd started in on what had to be done the next day.

"There are two reasons why it's important to do whatever we can to try to get your father released until his trial," he said. "First, it would mean a lot to him to be home and leading as normal a life as possible. Jail isn't an easy place for a person to be, as I'm sure you can imagine, and to be frank, I think your father is having a difficult time with it."

"What do you mean?" Aunt Cynthia asked.

Mr. Brubaker gave her a solemn look before continuing, and then he didn't answer her question. "Second, if your father were home, it would help his case. If we can get him out on bail, that gives the jury, once it's selected, the idea that he isn't dangerous, because if he *were*, he'd still be locked up. If, on the other hand, we don't get him out on bail, well, suffice it to say that the jury will be left with an entirely different impression. So it's very important, Tasha, that you look directly at your father during the proceedings tomorrow. Look at him as if you believe in him — "

"Of course I believe in him," Tasha snapped. Mr. Brubaker might be a good lawyer, as her father had said, but Tasha wasn't sure she liked him. Nor was she sure that *he* believed in her father. Even Aunt Cynthia seemed taken aback by his somewhat slick manner.

Mr. Brubaker smiled. "That's the girl," he said. "That's exactly the attitude I want to see. Of *course* you believe in your father. He's innocent. Why shouldn't you believe in him? That's important, Tasha. If the judge sees that there's no doubt in your mind, that you support your father, it can be a big help. Now then, let's talk wardrobe."

"Wardrobe?" Tasha wasn't sure she understood.

"Clothes make the man," Mr. Brubaker said. "Or, in this case, the young woman. You want your clothes tomorrow to say to the judge, 'I'm a reliable, responsible, trustworthy member of this society. I'm someone who was brought up right by a caring, loving father. I'm someone whose opinion you should trust, and my opinion is that my father is innocent.' "

"In that case, maybe she should wear a message T-shirt," Aunt Cynthia said wryly. "How about 'Let my daddy go'?"

Mr. Brubaker fixed her with a condescending gaze. "I hardly think that's constructive, Ms, er . . ." He consulted a pad of legal paper on which he had scrawled pages of notes. "*Miss* Jarvis. You should be setting a positive example for Natasha. And by the way, I'm also expecting you to show up tomorrow and to look equally supportive. Now then," he turned back to Tasha, "I want to see you in a dress. You do own a dress, don't you?"

"I have a couple."

"Something simple," Mr. Brubaker said. "Conservative. I don't want to see anything too short, or any plunging necklines. Dark colours are best. With stockings and appropriate shoes."

"You make it sound like she's going to a funeral," Aunt Cynthia said.

"That is precisely what I'm trying to avoid, Miss Jarvis." Mr. Brubaker dropped his legal pad into his leather briefcase, snapped the catch shut and stood up.

"Court is at ten o'clock tomorrow morning. Plan to arrive five or ten minutes early. And don't worry, Tasha. We're going to do our best to have your father home with you tomorrow night."

* * *

Tasha watched her father being led into the courtroom, and thought it was the hardest thing she would have to do all day. He looked smaller than she remembered. With his shoulders slumped and his face so pale, he looked older too. Could anything be more difficult, she wondered, than seeing him so miserable and not being able to jump up and rush over to him and hug him? She might have done it anyway, except that Mr. Brubaker turned and gave her a solemn warning look, and then Aunt Cynthia touched her arm lightly, just enough to remind her of the gravity of the situation. She must not under any circumstances do anything that would hurt her father's chances.

She followed Mr. Brubaker's instructions to the letter. Not once did she take her eyes from her father. She saw the glow of hope on his face when Denny Durant said he'd be willing to put up the money to get him out, that Leonard Scanlan was a respected businessman and that it was ridiculous to

127

think that he would try to flee the country. She saw his hope waver when, under the grilling of the crown attorney, Denny had to admit that the Lenny and Denny restaurants had suffered badly during the prolonged recession, that he and Leonard had had to mortgage two of the locations and that, yes, he supposed a man carrying a high debt load had less reason to stay in town than one who owned a going concern. She saw that hope vanish when a man she'd never seen before, an accountant, said that Leonard had told him only a few months ago that he was considering throwing in the towel, just walking away from the restaurants. Finally, when a cook from the Lenny and Denny's in the west end said that Leonard Scanlan had an explosive temper and had physically threatened him on more than one occasion, despair flooded her father's face and Tasha had to look away.

The crown attorney went on to speak at length about the case against Leonard Scanlan. She argued that Leonard Scanlan was a dangerous man who had brutally murdered his wife and whose crime had gone undetected for years, thanks to his duplicitous nature and keen criminal mind. His financial difficulties gave him all the more reason to flee were he released on bail. He should therefore be kept behind bars until his trial.

When the crown attorney had finished Mr. Brubaker got up. He turned and smiled at Tasha before he began his argument. Leonard Scanlan was not a dangerous man, he said. Sure, he might have a quick temper, but prior to being arrested, he had never been in any trouble with the law. As to the possibility of his fleeing, well, he disagreed that there was any danger there.

"Mr. Scanlan is a respected member of this community. He has a business to run. Yes, it's been a struggle. But Mr. Scanlan isn't the only business-man who's been hard pressed by difficult economic times. In fact, keeping him in jail is impeding his ability to look after his business interests. Then there's the matter of Mr. Scanlan's daughter, Your Honour." He turned to Tasha again. "Her mother has been murdered. The poor child is traumatized. She needs her father. She needs some sense of normalcy in her life if she is to weather this storm. Keeping her father locked up will hurt this girl. It will hurt Mr. Scanlan. And it will do nothing at all to advance the cause of justice."

Mr. Brubaker spoke more about Leonard Scan-lan's good record, cross-examined the cook who had called him violent, and called in others from his staff to testify to his character. Through it all Tasha watched her father's grim face. When Mr. Brubaker sat down, silence overtook the court.

Tasha sat tall, gazing at her father just she had been instructed, but she stole a glance at the judge from time to time. His deliberations seemed to take an eternity. What was the stern-faced judge think-ing? Was he more swayed by the arguments of the crown attorney, or would he accede to Mr. Brubaker's reasoning?

Finally the judge looked up. Tasha's eyes were fixed on her father, whose head had been bowed and who had been staring down at the floor and thinking . . . well, she could only imagine what he'd been thinking. She knew what wild thoughts would have been racing through her mind if she were in his place. Mr. Brubaker straightened in his chair. Aunt Cynthia laid a hand on Tasha's arm.

"The court is sympathetic to the argument made by Mr. Brubaker," the judge began, "especially to the circumstances of the accused's daughter — " he paused to look at Tasha for a moment " — and acknowledges that normalcy would undoubtedly be in her best interests."

Tasha held her breath. So far so good, she thought. It sounded as if he'd found Mr. Brubaker's argument more convincing than the crown attorney's. Her father wasn't some crazy butcher. He was a chef, a good man, a man who'd never done anything wrong in his whole life. Surely they'd have to let him go free until his trial. They couldn't possibly intend to treat him like some psycho axe murderer who had to be locked up for the good of society.

"However," the judge said.

However, a word that signalled the thwarting of hope. Tasha's heart sank. She saw her father's shoulders sag. He seemed to age before her eyes and, watching him, she could barely concentrate on what the judge was saying. Words collided with each other, like glass in a kaleidoscope — brutal nature of the crime, violent temperament, strength of the crown's case, flight risk. The picture they made filled Tasha with hopelessness. She heard the judge name a trial date. It echoed, as if he had shouted it from the edge of a bottomless chasm. Tasha stared at her father, who was slumped for-

ward in his chair as if he'd been knocked uncon-
scious. Her heart ached for him. She started to go to
him, but Aunt Cynthia held her back.

"He'll be okay," she whispered. "Don't do anything rash, Tasha."

Then the judge was turning his attention to the
next case and her father was being helped to his feet
by Mr. Brubaker and one of the court officers and,
before Tasha had a chance to say anything to him,
he was led from the courtroom, back to jail.

* * *

Tasha lifted her head off her pillow and listened just
long enough to recognize Jace's voice and to understand that he was talking to Aunt Cynthia.

"But I promised I'd pick her up," he was saying.
"I think she'd want to see me."

"I told you, Tasha is sleeping," Aunt Cynthia
said firmly.

For once her steely tone didn't annoy Tasha.
She was glad Aunt Cynthia was out there guarding
the door like a well-trained Doberman. She didn't
want to see anyone or talk to anyone, not even Jace.
What was the point? Everyone thought her father
was guilty. Even the judge considered him too dangerous to turn loose while the wheels of justice
turned. Whatever happened to "innocent until
proven guilty"? she wondered. As far as the whole
world was concerned, her father was already tried
and convicted. Who was she, one person — a kid,
at that — to change their minds?

"Look, I promised Tasha I'd pick her up and
take her downtown," Jace said. His voice was closer
now. "When I make a promise — especially a

promise to Tasha — I keep it, okay?"

"Look here, young man — "

They sounded as if they were right outside Tasha's door now. She sat up, wiping tears and sleep from her eyes, just as someone started to hammer on her door. Then she heard a thump, as if someone had crashed into it. Tasha leapt up off her bed and hurried to the door to open it. Jace tumbled in backwards. Tasha caught him before he fell. Aunt Cynthia, looking alarmed, rushed forward as he toppled.

"Are you okay?" Tasha asked him.

Jace gazed at Tasha as he righted himself. "Didn't mean to burst in on you," he said, "and if you don't want me here, just say the word and I'm gone."

"I thought you were sleeping," Aunt Cynthia said. "I thought you didn't want to be disturbed."

"It's okay," Tasha said. She hadn't been sleeping, she'd been crying. She'd felt so alone, as if no one in the world cared about her, and now here were these two people, peering at her, trying to gauge her mood, obviously caring a great deal. The sight of them cheered her a little.

"I forgot to tell you that Jace was coming over," Tasha said to her aunt. Then, to Jace, "I need a few minutes to get ready. Maybe if you ask her nicely, Aunt Cynthia will give you a couple of her white-chocolate-and-macadamia-nut cookies. She's a fabulous cook, you know." She smiled at her aunt, who looked relieved.

"This way, Jason," she said, and the two of them headed for the kitchen while Tasha retreated back to her room to change out of the navy blue dress she was still wearing from court.

Once they were in his car Jace said, "Your aunt told me what happened. I'm sorry it turned out the way it did. I was really hoping they'd let him out on bail. We all were."

"*We?*"

"My parents and me. Kids at school. People."

Tasha shook her head slowly. "You mean there are people at school who think my father is innocent?"

Jace looked surprised. "Sure," he said. "There *are* some who think he did it, but they're just stupid. They think just because a person gets arrested, he's guilty. They haven't figured out that you have to hear all the facts of the case before you make up your mind. That's what trials are for, right?"

"Right," Tasha said. She was still digesting the fact that there were people out there who didn't think her father belonged behind bars.

"Whew," Jace muttered as they stood in the crowded office of the Registrar General. "Talk about a nightmare of municipal bureaucracy. I count nine people behind the counter, and only one wicket open."

They had to wait in line for nearly an hour just to get some information about how to go about getting the information they really needed. When they finally reached the head of the line and Tasha explained what she was looking for, the woman behind the counter said, "Can't help you," then looked over Tasha's shoulder to the person behind her and said, "Next!"

Tasha didn't budge. "What do you mean, you can't help me?"

"I mean, that information is confidential," the woman said impatiently. "If you want, you can have a search done so see if we have the information. But all it will tell you is whether we have a record of that person's marriage. Any specific information about that person is confidential. We can't release it except to the person involved."

"That doesn't make any sense," Jace said. "Why would someone want to do a search to find out who her own husband is?"

The woman behind the counter gave Jace a withering look. "There are laws regarding confidentiality," she explained.

"But I thought marriages were a matter of public record," Jace argued.

"Well," the woman snapped, "you're wrong."

This was crazy. "There must be some way to find out what someone changed their name to."

"If they *officially* changed their name," the woman said slowly, "there'd be a record of that."

Aha! Tasha thought. "When someone gets married and takes her husband's name, that's an official name change, isn't it?"

"It could be," the woman said. "*If* they do it officially. A lot of people don't. Many just assume their husband's name. In that case, there are no records."

"So looking at name change records wouldn't help us, is that what you're saying?"

The woman nodded.

Jace looked completely exasperated. "This is ridiculous — "

Tasha pulled him away from the counter.

"Maybe there's another way," she said.

"Like?"

Tasha shrugged. "The public library?" She checked her watch. "We can still make it if we hurry."

The reference librarian was friendlier than the clerk at the Registrar General's office, but not much more help. "Do you know exactly when this person got married?" she asked.

Tasha had to shake her head. "Three or four years ago," she said, then added, "I think."

"Do you know anyone who was at the wedding? Maybe they'd be able to help you."

Another shake of the head.

"I thought," Tasha said, "that there must be some way we could do an on-line search of the newspaper. I thought if there was an announcement of her wedding — "

"I'm afraid that won't work," the librarian said. "Newspapers put a lot of their information on-line, but there's still a lot they *don't* put on-line — births, deaths, marriages, advertisements. Besides, the major dailies carry birth and death announcements, but engagements and marriages are generally found in the local weeklies. They're pretty small and aren't likely to have put anything on-line."

Tasha groaned. "Are you saying there's no way to locate the information I'm looking for?"

"No fast way," the librarian said. "You can try looking at our newspaper microfilm. It would take a while, but if there's a notice of engagement or a wedding announcement, chances are you'll find it."

Tasha glanced at Jace, who shrugged. "Okay," she said to the librarian. "How do we do that?"

"Well, you come back tomorrow — "

"*Tomorrow*?"

The librarian offered an apologetic smile. "We close in ten minutes," she said. "But if you come back tomorrow, someone will be glad to show you know to handle the microfilm."

"Well," Jace said as they left the library together, "I guess I know what I'm doing tomorrow morning."

"What about school?"

He shrugged. "What about it?"

* * *

They were standing in front of the library the next morning before the doors opened. A librarian showed them where to locate the microfilm; another showed them how to load the machine and read the reels.

"How hard can this be?" Jace said.

Tasha looked dubiously at the reel she was loading onto a microfilm reader. "I don't know," she said. "They sure pack a lot of information onto these things. And even if she was married somewhere around here, that still means looking through a bunch of weekly papers. This could end up being a lot more complicated than it sounds."

Jace laughed. "We're looking for a pretty straightforward piece of information," he said. "How long could it take?"

In fact, it took hours. And then it wasn't Tasha who found it. It was Jace.

"Eureka!" he said, so loudly that several people

in the microfilm room glared at him. "Look," he whispered to Tasha. "Look at this."

She got up and peered over his shoulder at the screen. There, in the middle of a page of wedding photos and engagement notices, were the few short lines that gave her the name she needed: Herbert Frederick Marcuse. Lucille Horstbueller had married Herbert Marcuse who, at the time the notice had appeared in the paper, lived in North York.

"You don't suppose he still lives there, do you?" Jace asked.

Tasha had been wondering the same thing. She glanced around, spotted a bank of pay phones near the library exit, and headed straight for it. Jace trotted along behind her.

Mara . . . Marborough . . . Marchant . . . Marcus . . . Marcuse, A. . . . Marcuse, C. . . . Marcuse, George . . . "He's here!" Tasha said. "Herbert Frederick Marcuse. 1913 Hyacinth Crescent."

Jace looked as excited as she was. "What are we waiting for?"

Chapter Eleven

Tasha sat in the front seat of Jace's car, a map book open on her lap, staring across the street at a two-storey stone house set in the middle of a neatly kept yard. The brass numbers beside the bright blue door read 1913.

"There it is," Tasha said. All things considered, it had been remarkably easy to locate Herbert Marcuse.

"Yup," Jace agreed. "There it is." He started to get out of the car.

"Wait," Tasha cried. "Where are you going?"

"To talk to Evart Horstbueller's daughter," Jace said. He frowned at her. "Is something wrong, Tash? I thought the whole point was to find out if Lucille Horstbueller knows anything about what happened that night."

"Ye-es," Tasha said, "but . . . "

"But what?"

"N-nothing, I guess." Nothing, and everything.

There, right in front of her, was Herbert Marcuse's house. Herbert Marcuse had married Lucille Horstbueller. It was possible — remotely possible, Tasha supposed, now that she was confronted with it — that Evart Horstbueller had been at the Fireside Café that night and had seen Catherine Scanlan arrive. He may have known whether or not she was alone. If she was with someone, he may have known who that person was, and have said something about it to his daughter Lucille when she picked him up to drive him home.

Until this precise moment, all of Tasha's hopes had been riding on finding Lucille Horstbueller and discovering what, if anything, her father had told her. Now that she was actually on the verge of that discovery, though, she suddenly felt like a player in a game of high stakes poker. Her whole future depended on what happened next. If she drew the wrong card and lost — if it turned out that Lucille Horstbueller knew nothing about what had happened that night — that was the end of the game. She had no other chance to win the jackpot — her father's freedom — short of Mrs. Mercer recovering from her injury and agreeing to tell the truth. If the cards were against her, there was nothing else for Tasha to hope for, no more reason to believe that she could prove her father innocent when everyone else seemed determined to prove the opposite.

"If you want," Jace said softly, "you can stay here and I'll go talk to her. I don't mind."

Good old Jace. Lately there didn't seem much that he wasn't prepared to do for her. But Tasha refused to let him handle this particular chore. Like it or not, it was something she had to do herself.

"No, it's okay," she said. "I'll be all right." She drew in a deep breath and pushed the car door open. Her legs trembled as she put her weight on them. She stood on the pavement, staring up at the house for a few moments, then turned back and stooped to peer back inside the car. "I wouldn't mind a little moral support, though," she said with a wan smile.

Jace was out of the car and standing beside her in a flash. Together they made their way up the flagstone walk and climbed the stone steps to the front door. Tasha forced herself to breathe slowly and regularly — in, two, three, four; out, two, three, four — to calm herself. She pressed the doorbell and waited.

No answer.

She glanced at Jace, who shrugged and pressed the button again.

Seconds ticked by.

Tasha was just about to turn away when a face flashed in the small window. The door swung open.

"Well, it's about time," said a woman who Tasha recognized immediately. Mrs. Marcuse was a slightly older version of Lucille Horstbueller, and she looked with apparent annoyance at Jace. "The first thing you need to know about me, Mr. Simmons, is that my lessons always start on time. If yours is scheduled to start at four-thirty, you should be ringing this bell at four-twenty-five. The second thing you need to know," and here she paused to turn blazing eyes on Tasha, "is that when you come for your lesson, you leave your girlfriend at home. However, since she's here this time, she can come in and wait in the foyer while you show me what you can do. Come on, hurry up, I haven't got all day. You're not my only student, you know. In fact, unless you can convince me that you have something for me to work with, you may not be my student at all."

She stood aside to let Tasha and Jace in, then guided Jace through the front hall into a large sunny room dominated by a grand piano. As he was hurried inside Jace looked back over his shoulder at Tasha and mouthed a single word: "Help."

Tasha scurried after him and reached the entrance to the practice room just as Mrs. Marcuse started to close the door. She gave Tasha a stern look. "I believe I said you were to wait in the foyer."

"We're not here for piano lessons," Tasha said.

Mrs. Marcuse looked puzzled. She turned to Jace. "Aren't you Albert Simmons?"

"Jace Bhupal," Jace said.

"If you're not here for lessons, then what do you want?"

"Actually," Tasha said, "we were hoping we could ask you a few questions about your father."

"My father?" Mrs. Marcuse repeated. She peered at Tasha. "Who are you?"

"My name is Natasha Scanlan," Tasha said. "Your father used to work at the Fireside Café when it belonged to my parents. My mother — "

"Tasha?" Mrs. Marcuse stared at her as if she were confronting a ghost. "Little Tasha Scanlan?"

Tasha nodded. "I don't know if you've heard what happened to my father — "

Mrs. Marcuse nodded solemnly. "Is that why

you're here?" she asked. "Because of your father?"

"Yes. You see — we — I was hoping that maybe you might know something about what happened the night my mother disappeared."

"Me?" Mrs. Marcuse looked astonished. "What could I possibly know?"

"I remember you used to come and pick your father up every night after work. I thought maybe he — "

"My father is dead," Mrs. Marcuse said. She spoke the words sharply, as if Tasha were somehow to blame for this fact. "He died a few years ago."

"Yes, I know," Tasha said. "And I'm sorry. But I thought perhaps he might have said something to you about what happened that night. My mother must have gone to the Café. That's where she was found."

"Are you saying that my father had something to do with what happened to your mother?" Mrs. Marcuse's voice was shrill now. Her face had turned red.

"No!" Tasha said, mortified at being misunderstood. "No, not at all. I just thought that if your father had noticed anything, if he'd seen my mother when she arrived at the Café, he might have said something to you. He might have had some idea who wanted to kill her — "

Mrs. Marcuse's eyes hardened. "I don't know anything about it," she said. "It's because of your mother that — " She broke off suddenly. "Please," she said. "I'm expecting a student any moment."

But Tasha couldn't go. Somebody had to know something. It wasn't possible that no one had seen anything.

"Your father liked my mother," she said. "I know he did."

Mrs. Marcuse's eyes glistened with barely contained tears.

"Please," Tasha begged. "Please just think about it for a minute. Maybe he said something, anything at all, that might help to prove that my father is innocent. Please, Mrs. Marcuse. If there's anything at all that the police might be able to follow up on — "

"The police? What are they — Are you saying the police are going to turn up on my doorstep next?"

"We'd sure like that to happen," Jace said.

Mrs. Marcuse turned on him, her eyes wild. "What do you mean? Are you accusing *me* of something?"

"No, not at all," Tasha said quickly. "He only meant that if there was anything you remember, anything at all that might be of interest to the police, that could help my father."

"I'm sorry," Mrs. Marcuse said. Her voice was cold. "As I've already said, I know nothing. Now if you'll excuse me . . . " She crossed the foyer and swung open the front door. "I'm afraid I'll have to ask you to leave." When Tasha opened her mouth to plead her case further Mrs. Marcuse said, "Right now, please, before I have to call the police myself and have them escort you off my property."

Shaking with indignation and disappointment Tasha followed Jace down the Marcuses' flagstone walk. She turned to look back up at the stone house while Jace unlocked the car door for her. Mrs.

143

Marcuse had gone inside and the house looked quiet, except for a slight fluttering of the curtains in the living room. Tasha was sure Mrs. Marcuse was standing behind them, waiting for her and Jace to leave. She turned, got into the car and buckled her seat belt. They drove for a few blocks, then Jace pulled over and stopped the car.

"What's the matter?" Tasha asked. "Why are you stopping?"

"For a post mortem."

"A *what*?"

"A post mortem. You know, an examination of the facts, after the fact. Was it just me, or did Lucille Horstbueller, a.k.a. Mrs. Herbert Marcuse, become extremely agitated when you asked her about her father?"

"She sure did," Tasha agreed. "But in a way I guess you can't blame her." She was being more generous than she felt. She desperately wanted to blame the woman for something. "She really iced up when you mentioned the police might want to talk to her, though."

"Yeah," Jace answered. "Maybe that wasn't the smartest thing to say."

Tasha shrugged, still pondering. Not only had Lucille Marcuse been unhelpful, she had been unfriendly. She had even threatened them. Still, when Tasha thought about it, she had to admit that under the same circumstances, she might have reacted the same way. "What would you do if someone you hadn't seen in five years suddenly showed up on your doorstep and started asking about your deceased father? You'd probably get a little agitated, too."

"Maybe." Jace thought about this for a minute. "But I doubt I'd threaten to have the police throw that person off my property. *That* was an extreme reaction."

"For all we know, Mrs. Marcuse is an extreme person."

"That's one possibility. Do you remember her being that way when she'd come to drop off her father?"

"No, not really, but I didn't know her very well. Do you have some theory?"

"Maybe," Jace said. "Sometimes people get upset when they're caught in a lie. And was it just me, or did she seem to have some kind of grudge against your mother, almost as if she blamed her in some way for her father's death?"

"What are you saying? That she was lying to us? That Evart Horstbueller killed my mother?"

Jace shrugged. "It's possible, isn't it? Just because a person is dead, that doesn't mean he didn't do something nasty while he was still alive. I mean, when you think about it, there's no law that says a murderer can't die before being brought to justice."

"True," Tasha admitted. She hadn't considered that possibility. "But suppose you're right. Suppose Evart Horstbueller is the murderer — or *was* the murderer — why would his daughter be upset five years later, *after* his death?"

Jace shrugged. "Remember what Enrico Zapata said, that maybe Evart Horstbueller's death wasn't an accident? He was hinting at suicide."

"You mean that maybe Evart Horstbueller killed my mother and then killed himself afterward, in remorse?"

"It's possible."

Tasha pondered this. "I don't know," she said. "Besides, it just doesn't make sense that he did it. He liked my mother. They got along great."

"So you think Mrs. Marcuse acted strangely just because you popped up out of the blue and started asking questions about her dear old long-gone dad, and that it doesn't mean anything that she definitely seemed to have some kind of grudge against your mother?"

"I didn't say *that*." Tasha sighed. This was getting more complicated, just when she wanted it to be getting simpler. She wished the last few minutes had turned out differently. She wished that instead of becoming first upset and then hostile, Lucille Horstbueller Marcuse had instead spilled out the secrets that had been hidden for five years: *Now that you mention it, Tasha, my father did say something about your mother coming to the restaurant the night of the big storm. No, she wasn't alone. She was with someone. A man, my father said. A rather nasty man. His name? Let me think a minute. Yes, my father did say that he knew the man. As I recall, he said his name was —*

"Well, well, well," Jace muttered. "Will you look at that."

Tasha turned just in time to see a grass green convertible speed by. Behind the wheel was Lucille Marcuse. Instead of braking for the STOP sign ahead, she merely slowed a fraction, then cruised right through the intersection.

"It looks like she's in a big hurry," Tasha said.

Jace flicked on his turn signal and pulled out

into traffic. "Too much of a hurry for someone who was expecting a piano student to show up at any minute," he said. "Suppose we find out where she's going."

"That's exactly what I was thinking." Tasha sat forward in her seat, straining against her seat belt to keep track of the green convertible. "She's turning up at the light. Making a left."

By the time Jace reached the intersection the light had turned red.

"Rats!" He slapped the steering wheel.

"I can still see her," Tasha said. "Up ahead. There isn't much traffic." But by the time the light had changed and Jace was able to make his turn, the green convertible had vanished. Jace drove around for a few minutes anyway, hunting without luck for Mrs. Marcuse's car.

"It was probably nothing," he said when he finally gave up the chase.

"You really think so?"

He looked at Tasha for a very long time before answering. "Truthfully?"

"Truthfully."

"I think Mrs. Marcuse's reaction was too extreme for it to be nothing. And when we arrived at her house she was clearly expecting a student — she thought I was him. But before that student had a chance to show up she jumped into her car and roared off, driving a whole lot faster than you'd expect a piano teacher to drive. I think there's something else going on, Tasha, something that would explain such odd behaviour."

"But what?" Tasha asked. She wanted nothing

better than to agree with Jace, and would have given anything to prove that Mrs. Marcuse's behaviour had something to do with her mother's disappearance five years ago. If only there was some way to be sure that Mrs. Marcuse was really acting out of character . . . Tasha snapped her fingers. "We have to go back to her house," she said.

"What for?"

"Please, Jace, just do it. Right now."

Jace shrugged, but turned the car around and headed back.

As he drove Tasha wondered whether they were onto something, or whether they were merely grasping at straws. She glanced back over her shoulder, half-expecting to see Mrs. Marcuse's car appear, heading innocently home again.

"Hey!" she said in surprise.

"Hey what?"

Trailing a few car lengths behind them was a black T-bird, and for a moment Tasha was sure she recognized the driver. "Isn't that the same car that almost rear-ended you near Mrs. Mercer's place?" What was it doing here?

"What car?" Jace said.

Tasha looked behind them again, just in time to see the T-bird make a left turn and disappear from sight.

"Funny," she murmured.

"What's funny?"

"For a minute there, I thought we were being followed."

Jace shrugged. "It was probably just a coincidence. Maybe it wasn't even the same car."

"Maybe," Tasha said. Probably, she thought. There must be hundreds of black T-birds in the city.

When they reached Lucille Marcuse's big stone house Jace parked halfway down the block from it. "Now what?" he said.

"Now we wait."

"For?"

Tasha wasn't sure. "We just need to eliminate a few possibilities," she said. "Hey, look." She pointed at the Marcuse house. A boy about Jace's age was plodding up the flagstone path.

"Albert Simmons?" Jace said.

"I'd be willing to bet on it."

They watched the boy ring the doorbell, wait, and ring it again. And again. After the third time he jumped down from the steps and crossed the lawn to try to look into the big picture window, but without apparent success. Back he went up the walk and up the steps to ring the bell again. Finally he headed down to the sidewalk, turning every few steps to look at the house. He seemed quite perplexed.

"Can we go," Jace asked, "or are we waiting for something in particular?"

"We're just waiting," Tasha said.

A half hour passed, and another person turned up the flagstone path, this one a girl who looked about eleven or twelve. She did more or less the same thing that Albert Simmons had done, but had a big smile on her face as she finally turned and skipped down the path to the sidewalk.

"Obviously not someone who looks forward to her weekly piano lesson," Jace said.

149

Precisely thirty minutes later another child appeared, rang, hammered on the front door, rang some more and left.

"Mrs. Marcuse struck me as someone who takes her job seriously," Tasha said. "Someone who is very demanding with her pupils. You heard what she said — she expected them to turn up five minutes early for their lessons."

"You would have thought she'd practise what she preaches," Jace said.

"Exactly. She took off because of something we said, I'd be willing to bet on that too."

"But where did she go?" Jace asked.

"Maybe to warn someone."

"Who? And why not just phone them? That should be easier than taking off like a bat out of hell. I don't get it."

"Neither do I," Tasha had to admit. "But she's the only lead we've come up with."

"Do we go?" Jace asked. "Or do we wait here a little longer?"

"We wait," Tasha said. "Maybe she went to pick up the person she had to talk to. Maybe she'll bring him — or her — back here."

"We should be so lucky. Maybe she got a phone call right after we left. Maybe there's been some sort of accident. Maybe her husband was hurt or something — "

Another girl trudged up the walk and rang the bell. While she waited for an answer a car pulled into the Marcuse driveway and a man in a dark suit got out. He waved to the girl, who said something to him. The man frowned. He produced a key from his pocket and fitted it into the front lock.

"That must be Mr. Marcuse," Jace said.

Mr. Marcuse pushed the door open and went inside. A moment later he was out on the steps again, looking puzzled as he alternately talked to the girl and glanced at a piece of paper in his hand. The girl shook her head. A few more words were exchanged, then the girl turned and walked down the path. Mr. Marcuse went out into the driveway and opened the garage door. He looked even more puzzled when he saw that it was empty.

"Let's go," Tasha said.

"Go?"

"It's time for you to be Albert Simmons. A very indignant Albert Simmons."

Jace looked completely baffled. "I don't get it."

"Come on," Tasha said. "I'll explain."

* * *

"Mrs. Marcuse isn't here?" Jace said to Mr. Marcuse. Tasha was impressed by how convincingly annoyed he managed to look and sound. "But how can she not be here? I have an appointment with her to discuss lessons. It was all arranged. She was very insistent that I arrive a few minutes early."

"Yes, I understand, Mr. . . . . er . . . ?"

"Simmons. Albert Simmons," Jace said, with just the right amount of stiffness. "I was under the impression that Mrs. Marcuse was a professional. I was told that she was a rigorous teacher."

"She *is*," Mr. Marcuse said. He seemed embarrassed to have to explain his wife's absence. "I'm sorry that you've been inconvenienced, but my wife has apparently been called away unexpectedly." He peered at the piece of paper in his hand as if it contained a great mystery. "I'll tell her you were here. I'll have her call you to arrange another appointment."

"You have no idea where she is?" Tasha asked. "Albert is leaving the country this evening for a few days. If we could call her before he goes — "

Mr. Marcuse was shaking his head. "I'm afraid there's no phone where Mrs. Marcuse is," he said. "But I'll have her call you the minute she returns. Really, I'm very sorry for the inconvenience."

When they were back in the car Jace turned to Tasha. "*Now* do we leave?" he asked. "I'm getting hungry."

"In a while," Tasha promised.

A while turned out to be nearly an hour and a half longer. The sun was sinking close to the horizon when Mrs. Marcuse's grass green convertible suddenly swung into sight. She parked in the driveway behind her husband's car and hurried into the house.

"Now can we go?" Jace asked again. "I'm starving."

"In a minute," Tasha said. She pushed open the car door.

"Where are you going?"

"I want to take a look at her car."

"What for?"

Tasha wasn't sure. Maybe there was something to be seen, something that would help her figure out where Mrs. Marcuse had gone. She jumped out of Jace's car, walked up the street as nonchalantly as possible, and slowed her pace when she reached the foot of the Marcuses' driveway. Then, glancing around and seeing no one, she sidled up to the green convertible for a closer look. She didn't find out much.

Her hands balled into fists at her sides. Something was definitely peculiar about the way Lucille Marcuse was acting. Even her husband seemed surprised by her odd behaviour. Where had she gone in such a hurry, and why had she been so upset? It was frustrating to have such a strong sense that something was wrong, and yet be unable to do anything to figure out exactly what. It was so frustrating that Tasha felt like kicking something — one of the convertible's tires, for instance. She might have if they hadn't all been covered with mud.

Chapter Twelve

Aunt Cynthia ran out the front door and was halfway down the walk before Jace even switched off his engine.

"Tasha, thank goodness," she cried. "I had no idea where you were."

Tasha hurried to meet her. Aunt Cynthia was turning out to be a real worrier. She got all worked up whenever she didn't know precisely where Tasha was. "Jace and I just went to talk to someone," she said. "A woman whose father used to work at the Café — "

"Oh, Tasha," Aunt Cynthia said, her voice anguished. "Your father — "

Tasha's stomach churned as she looked at her aunt's flushed face and troubled eyes. "What's wrong, Aunt Cynthia? What about Dad?"

"He's in the hospital."

Tasha's heart nearly stopped beating in her chest.

"They say it was some kind of accident," Aunt Cynthia continued, "but I don't know exactly what happened. They wouldn't give me any details."

"But he's okay, isn't he?" Tasha demanded. "It's not serious, is it?"

Jace twisted around in his seat to unlock the car's back door.

"Climb in, Ms Jarvis," he said. "I'll drive you both to the hospital."

An armed guard posted at the door to Leonard Scanlan's room refused to let Tasha enter until he had called the police station for instructions. Then he told her, "I'm afraid you're going to have to wait."

"Wait?" Tasha echoed in disbelief. Now that she was this close to her father, she didn't think she could stand to let even a few more seconds pass before seeing for herself how he was. "If my father's been hurt, I want to see him."

The police officer said he understood how she felt, but added, "You can't see him right now. Why don't you take a seat in the waiting room down the hall, and I'll let you know when you can go in."

Tasha wouldn't have budged if it hadn't been for Aunt Cynthia and Jace, who each took one of her arms and led her away. She was surprised to find Denny Durant pacing up and down in the small waiting room.

"What are you doing here?" she asked.

"The same thing you are. Waiting to see what's going on. The police were in my office when they got a call. Something's happened to your dad, kiddo, but they wouldn't tell me what."

Tasha sank down onto one of the plastic waiting room chairs and tried not to think the worst. It wasn't easy.

An impossibly long time passed before Detectives Pirelli and Marchand appeared. Mr. Brubaker was right behind them.

Tasha jumped up to meet them. "What's happened?" she demanded. "Why can't I see my father?"

"You can," Detective Marchand said, "in a minute. But we wanted to see you first, before you went in, so you'll be prepared."

Tasha looked wildly at Aunt Cynthia, who asked sharply, "What's that supposed to mean? What's happened to Leonard?"

Detective Marchand surprised Tasha by looking to Mr. Brubaker for help. The lawyer said sombrely, "Maybe you'd better sit down, Natasha."

Tasha felt her knees give way. *Maybe you'd better sit down* was what people said on TV or in movies just before they made some terrible announcement, like someone had been diagnosed with a terminal illness, or had died. She held onto Jace's arm to steady herself.

"I think she'd rather stand," Jace said.

Mr. Brubaker didn't argue. "Your father . . . well, as I'm sure you can imagine, he's been depressed about this whole situation. He's been worried about you and about how his restaurants are faring."

"What about them?" Denny Durant asked. "I'm handling things now." He sounded insulted.

"They aren't in the best of financial health as it

156

is," Mr. Brubaker said. "Leonard has been worried that his arrest will lead to the restaurants going under."

Tasha waited for Denny to contradict the lawyer, but he didn't.

"It *has* been tough lately," Denny said. "But I'd never let the chain go under. No way."

Tasha had heard her father say on more than one occasion that Denny knew nothing about the business end of running a restaurant. No wonder he was worried.

Mr. Brubaker turned back to Tasha. "He's also worried about you, Tasha, about how all of this has affected you. I'm afraid he feels responsible — "

"*Responsible*?" Tasha echoed. "You mean you think he did it?"

Mr. Brubaker shook his head. "No. No. What I mean is that he regrets fighting with your mother and letting her leave that night. He regrets not supporting her in her desire to get away from the restaurant business for a while." He studied Tasha a moment. "I'm afraid there's no easy way to say this, Tasha. It seems your father tried to kill himself."

If it weren't for Jace's sure grip, Tasha would have collapsed. But Jace backed her into one of the plastic waiting room chairs and held her until she sank down onto it. The whole room spun around her as she grappled with what Mr. Brubaker had said. She tried to imagine the despair her father must have felt to be driven to such an act. His anguish had been written on his face the last time she'd seen him. If only he'd been released on bail. She was sure that if he were at home awaiting trial instead of being locked up in a jail cell, things would be easier for him.

"How is he?" she asked slowly. "Did he . . . did he hurt himself badly?"

"No," Mr. Brubaker said. "Someone noticed what was happening before it went too far. But he has been sedated, and they want to keep him here overnight for observation."

"Can I see him?"

"Of course," Detective Marchand said. "We just wanted you to know what happened first. Of course you can see him."

Tasha felt as if she were being carried through the hospital corridors on legs that were not her own. Everything seemed so unreal — her passage down the hall, the jerky movement of the police officer outside her father's room as he stood up and opened the door for her, the cold touch of Aunt Cynthia's hand on her arm as she went through the door with Tasha, the utter drabness of the hospital room which, Tasha saw, had bars on its one drearily small window.

Leonard Scanlan lay on the crisp hospital sheets, his eyes closed, his face as pale as the pillowcase. He looked smaller than Tasha remembered, and she guessed that he hadn't been eating well these past few days, but other than that she could see no sign of any injury. She crept toward the bed and touched his hand. It was reassuringly warm.

"Dad?"

His eyes fluttered open, and immediately filled with tears. "Tasha — "

"It's okay, Dad," Tasha whispered, her own cheeks suddenly wet. She wiped at her tears and tried to look brave. "It's okay." She leaned over her father and hugged him, and was reassured to find that his grip was strong and tight. When she pulled back, she noticed for the first time something odd on his neck, a red mark that seemed to run round it, almost as if —

Suddenly her father raised his hand and jerked on the neckline of his hospital gown, covering the mark.

"How are you feeling, Dad?" Tasha asked. "Are you okay?"

Leonard Scanlan gave a slight nod. "Tasha, I'm sorry. I just — " His voice dropped to a whisper. "You have no idea what it's like in there, Tasha."

"I know," she said, although she could barely imagine what his life must have been like since his arrest.

"There's something else, Tasha," he said. "Something I hoped you'd never have to worry about — "

"If you're concerned about your restaurants, Leonard," Aunt Cynthia said, stepping forward, "I'd be glad to see what I can do. I know a thing or two about the food service business, you know."

Leonard Scanlan looked with gratitude at his sister-in-law. "Would you?" he asked.

"I'd be glad to. And don't worry about Tasha, either. She's a good kid. Strong and determined. She'll be fine."

Another tear rolled down Leonard Scanlan's cheek. He held tightly to Tasha's hand.

"Sit down, little one," he said. "Stay with me a while."

Tasha glanced over at Detective Marchand, who was standing in the doorway. The detective nodded. Tasha pulled a chair up close to the bed and sat down, holding her father's hand in her own.

When it came time to leave Tasha didn't want to go. Why wouldn't they let her stay with her father for the night? Why did she have to leave him there all alone? She wouldn't have minded sitting up in a chair all night. She would have stood on one foot from dusk to dawn if it would have helped to make her father feel better. But a nurse claimed that staying would be against hospital policy, and Detective Marchand told Tasha that her father was for all practical purposes still in custody. Besides, she pointed out gently, he was sound asleep. Tasha kissed her father's sunken cheek and followed the detective back out into the corridor.

Aunt Cynthia was in the waiting room, talking to Denny Durant. She got to her feet when she saw Tasha.

"I was just telling Denny what a determined young lady you are," she said, "and how you're doing everything you can to help your father."

"Where's Jace?" Tasha asked.

Aunt Cynthia shrugged. "He said he'd be back in a few minutes, but that was a while ago."

"I could give you a lift," Denny said.

"No thanks," Tasha replied. Maybe it wasn't fair, but she was angry with him. The whole time she'd been sitting with her father, she had imagined Denny talking to the police, telling them about her father's fiery temper. She reminded herself that Denny had appeared at the bail hearing, but it didn't help.

"I could call a taxi," Aunt Cynthia said.

"Did someone say taxi?" asked a voice behind Tasha. She turned to look at Jace's familiar face. "Sorry," he said. "I just thought that as long as we were here, I should check on Mrs. Mercer."

Tasha's heart raced. "How is she?" She felt Denny Durant's breath on the back of her neck as he stepped forward to hear the answer.

Jace's grim expression said it all. "No better, no worse," he said. "The nurses wouldn't tell me anything. But a woman in the next room — Mrs. Delvecchio, she's in for a hip replacement — told me she'd overheard a couple of nurse's aides talking. They said Mrs. Mercer could still come out of her coma, but it doesn't seem likely. How's your dad?"

Tasha shook her head.

"Come on," Jace said. "I'll drive you home."

* * *

Tasha sat in Jace's car long after Aunt Cynthia had gone into the house.

"You never did get anything to eat," she said. "I'm sorry."

"Don't be." He took her hand into his. "I grabbed a bite at the hospital cafeteria. You know, it's a miracle anyone ever comes out of hospital, considering the food that's shovelled into them while they're there. If you ask me, recovery in the face of such menacing menus is a testament to the human spirit." He smiled mischievously, then grew suddenly serious. "Pretty worried about your dad?"

Tasha's heart constricted when she thought of her father's pallor, and of the dull despair she had seen in his eyes. "I think . . . I'm afraid that he's given up," she whispered. "That scares me."

Jace said nothing. He waited until she was ready to speak again.

"I have to do *something*," she said. "I have to find a way to help him." She leaned back against the seat and peered out at the stars in the inky sky. "There was mud on her tires."

"Whose tires?"

"Mrs. Marcuse. Lucille. It hasn't rained for days, but when she got back from wherever she went, her tires were caked with mud."

Jace thought about this for a little while before saying, "It hasn't rained for weeks, never mind days. It hasn't rained anywhere in southern Ontario. How long was she gone, anyway?"

"Two and a half, maybe three hours."

"Which means maybe an hour and a quarter, an hour and a half each way, max." He thought about that for a few more moments. "She could have driven to a lake, maybe. That might account for the mud. Or maybe she was somewhere in farm country."

"Farm country?"

"Someplace north of the city maybe. Someplace where there might be irrigation, or a greenhouse operation of some kind. Or maybe — "

"Basically what you're saying is we have no idea where she went."

Jace shrugged. "Basically."

162

They were both silent as they considered this.

"But why?" Tasha asked. "Why would she suddenly take off like that? She didn't even call her students to cancel their lessons. She didn't call her husband, either. Why?"

"Remember what Mr. Marcuse said when we asked if we — if Arthur Simmons — could call to schedule another appointment? He said there was no phone where she was."

Tasha sat up straight and peered at him. "Are you thinking what I'm thinking? That she knows who did it? Or that she knows *someone* who knows something. And she went to warn that person that we were snooping around. That's possible, isn't it?"

"It sounds more than possible to me. It sounds like a pretty good explanation of why she acted so weird."

"If only there were some way we could find out exactly where she went and who she went to warn."

"Do you want to go back there tomorrow and talk to her again?" Jace asked.

"She didn't tell us what we wanted to know today. Why would she tomorrow? Unless — " An idea came half-formed into her mind. "Hey, you know that thing you're making for your grandmother?"

Jace grinned. "Yeah. Yeah, I think I'm following you."

Chapter Thirteen

Tasha glanced back over her shoulder, but couldn't see Jace's car, which was parked down the block. She sucked in a lungful of morning air, and wished that she hadn't chickened out of drama club tryouts back in eighth grade. Maybe if she'd had some stage experience, she'd be less nervous about what she was going to do now. Maybe she'd be able to stride confidently up the walk to the big stone house, rap authoritatively on the door, and say what she had to say with a convincing pretence of conviction. Maybe.

But she hadn't tried out for drama club. She'd been afraid her performance wouldn't fool anyone. After all, hadn't her father always told her she was a poor liar? "Your face gives it away, young lady," he'd say. "Take my advice and don't ever play poker for money. With a face as honest as yours, you'd lose every dime you bet."

Tasha wasn't playing this particular game for

anything as unimportant as money. The stakes were much higher. So high that her knees wobbled as she started up the flagstone walk.

Pull yourself together, she told herself. You can't afford to mess this up. If you don't convince Lucille Marcuse that you mean what you say, you'll lose the last chance you have to set your father free.

She forced herself to look straight ahead as she approached the bright blue door, even though the temptation to glance at the car in the driveway was overwhelming. Had Jace attached the device properly? Did it show? Would Lucille Marcuse notice it when she went out to her car — assuming Tasha could convince her to do just that? Maybe Lucille had seen Jace in her driveway earlier. Maybe she already suspected that something was about to happen.

Don't look, Tasha told herself. Don't look, don't think, just say your lines.

Sunlight glinted off the brass numbers bolted to the door frame. Tasha pressed the bell and waited.

Seconds ticked by. Sweat prickled the palms of her hands and under her arms. She reached for the doorbell again, but froze before she pressed it. The door swung open.

Lucille Marcuse, her face rigid with anger, stared out at her. "What are you doing here?" she demanded. "I told you I have nothing to say to you. I told you I'd call the police if you set foot on my property again. Don't think I won't."

Tasha's nervousness vanished, chased away by the sharpness of Lucille Marcuse's voice and eyes. Did she want to trade threats? Well, Tasha had one for her. "Go ahead and call them," she said. "I was going to give you a few hours, but if you want them here now, be my guest."

As Tasha had expected, her remarks baffled Lucille Marcuse. "What do you mean? What are you talking about?"

"I know where you went yesterday," Tasha said.

Lucille Marcuse stepped back into her house and began to close the door.

"My friend and I saw you leave the house," Tasha said. "We followed you."

Lucille Marcuse's face drained of colour. "In that case, why didn't you go to the police?" she said.

"Your father and my mother were friends, Mrs. Marcuse. Good friends. That's why I came to you first, to give you a chance the do the right thing. I want you to go to the police and tell them everything — "

"I'll do no such thing!" Mrs. Marcuse cried. "You can't prove anything."

"I'll give you three hours," Tasha said, and glanced at her watch. "Either you go to the police by noon and tell them everything, or I will. I'll tell them exactly where you went and who you were with. I'm sure they'll be very interested. I'm sorry about your father, Mrs. Marcuse, but *my* father is being blamed for a crime he didn't commit. I have to do everything I can to help him."

She turned then, without waiting for a response, and hurried back down the block in the opposite direction from where Jace sat waiting in his car. She felt Mrs. Marcuse's eyes on her as she kept walking, until finally she was well out of sight of the Marcuse

166

house. She waited for Jace in the place they had arranged.

Five minutes passed, then five more. What if Mrs. Marcuse didn't take the bait? What if she just went back inside her big beautiful house and sat down at her piano? What if the whole plan didn't work?

Tasha fretted as she paced on the sidewalk, unable to see what was happening at the Marcuse house. With each minute that passed, she became more convinced that their plan wasn't going to work. If it were, something would have happened by now.

Suddenly Jace's car swung into sight. Tasha ran toward it and hopped into the front seat.

"Did she go for it?"

"I think so. She jumped into her car a couple of minutes ago and took off. She was travelling well above the speed limit." He flipped up the screen of the laptop computer that sat on the front seat between him and Tasha. "Can you see her?"

A little white dot blipped on the screen.

"It looks like the radar in an air traffic control tower," she said. "Only better. I can see exactly where she is." Jace had overlaid a graphic program of the city map. "What happens if she goes over the edge of the map?"

"Depending on which direction she goes in, there's more map. Once she's outside city limits, though, we're more or less on our own. But there are fewer roads out there, fewer turns she could possibly take. We should be able to track her fairly easily. At least, that's the theory."

As Jace had predicted, following Mrs. Marcuse's car north through the city wasn't complicated. But then, abruptly, the little white Lucille Marcuse blip went shooting off the end of the map, and Tasha found herself trying to track it in relation to no familiar landmarks.

"Where are we anyway?" Tasha asked after staring at the blip on the computer screen for thirty minutes.

"We're just coming up on Holland Landing." Jace glanced at his watch. "If she's going to the same place as before, it can't be much farther. We've been on the road for nearly an hour."

"She's veering a little to the left," Tasha said.

"So is the road. Let me know if she makes any sudden turns."

She didn't. They kept on the two-lane road that carried them deeper and deeper into farm country. Then, without warning, the screen went dark.

"Something's wrong," Tasha howled. "Something's wrong!"

"Reboot it," Jace said, his voice calm. Tasha stared at him, flustered. "Roboot. It'll be fine."

She clicked `Control/Alt/Delete`, and heard the computer start to work again. Lights came on, the screen came clear.

"Now type in `map.exe`," Jace said.

Tasha typed. Suddenly the map and the little white blip were on the map again,

"Now," Jace said, still calm, "tell me where she is."

"East," Tasha said. "She's east of here, heading in a straight line."

Jace slowed the car.

"What are you doing?" Tasha asked, alarmed. "You're going to lose her."

"There's not much cover out here," Jace replied. "I can't afford to get too close."

Tasha looked around. The fields that spread out on either side of the road were either freshly cultivated or filled with only grass or clover, neither of which grew very high. Apart from the stands of trees that grew here and there between fields to break the wind, the land was flat enough so that she could see for long distances. Every now and again they passed a big grey or red barn and a stone farmhouse, although these stood mostly in the distance, down long concession roads.

"We have to be careful she doesn't see us, but at least we'll be able to see her," Jace said.

Tasha nodded. "It seems so peaceful out here," she said. Even the air had a freshness to it. She rolled her window down further and drew in a deep breath as they sped down the road. She was enjoying herself so much that she didn't notice right away that Mrs. Marcuse's grass green convertible was no longer travelling in the same direction.

"She's turned," Tasha cried. "She's made a sharp left."

"Keep your eyes peeled," Jace said. "There should be a road coming up soon."

Tasha leaned forward in her seat, straining against her seatbelt, so she could see past Jace to the left.

"There!" she cried at last. "There's a road." Then, as they got close, "I can see her car. At least,

I think I can." It had disappeared the moment she'd spied it.

Jace made the turn, and slowed the car even more as he travelled down this narrower road. "What do you see on the screen?"

"She made a sharp right up ahead," Tasha said. "Wait. Hey, it looks as if she's stopped." Then, "There's a farmhouse up ahead."

Jace tramped on the accelerator and the car shot ahead at twice the speed it had been travelling.

"What are you doing?" Tasha cried as they raced past an old farmhouse. Mrs. Marcuse's car was sitting in the yard in front of it.

"We're just two people Lucille Marcuse doesn't know, travelling to somewhere other than here," Jace said.

"Huh?"

"Tasha, if we stop right now, she'll see us. We'll never figure out what's going on."

"Good point," Tasha muttered.

They kept going until the road dipped a little, putting the farmhouse out of sight. Only then did Jace pull over.

"We're going to have to walk back," he said. "And we're going to have to be careful we're not seen."

They got out of the car and looked up the road.

"The quickest way is across those fields," Tasha said. There was a stand of maple and oak at the far end, close to the farmhouse. "If we try to stay behind those trees, we might be able to make it."

Jace nodded. They crouched to make themselves as small as possible, and hurried toward the trees. When they got there, they were only twenty or thirty metres from the farmyard where Mrs. Marcuse's car sat. They peered out from behind a thick-trunked oak as Lucille Marcuse disappeared into a rickety–looking barn.

"Whoever she came to warn must be inside," Tasha said.

Jace nodded again. "So," he said after a minute, "what do we do? March right in there and confront them? Or hang back and try to get a good look at whoever it is so we can tell the police?"

"Neither," Tasha said. "We need to find out who she came here to see. But if we can, we should also try to find out exactly what's going on, so we have something to tell the police."

Jace nodded. "Let's go," he said.

"*I'll* go," Tasha countered. "You stay here."

"But it might be dangerous."

"Which is exactly why you should stay here. If something's going to happen, it should happen to only one of us. That way the other one can go for help."

"Fine," Jace said. "Except that you stay here and I'll go find out what's happening — "

Tasha shook her head. "He's my father. I'm the one who has to do this." When Jace started to argue, she silenced him with a wave of her hand. "We're wasting time," she said. She glanced around, then stepped out from the cover of the oak.

"Be careful," Jace whispered behind her.

She held the words in her mind as she kept low and ran across the yard to the barn. She slowed as she got closer, and tiptoed the last few metres. When she reached the barn, she stopped and pressed her ear against the weather-beaten door. She heard nothing. She opened it a crack, and peeked in. Nothing but empty barn. Quickly she ducked inside, then stood holding her breath, listening.

Voices. She heard them dimly, and cocked an ear to guide her. Gradually the voices became more audible — she recognized one of them as Lucille Marcuse's. She was talking to a man.

"I'm telling you, you have to leave immediately," she said. "She knows. She's going to the police."

"If she knows, it's because you panicked," the male voice replied.

The man didn't sound angry. That puzzled Tasha. If she were in hiding and her hiding place had been jeopardized by someone else's stupidity she would have been furious. But this voice sounded merely tired.

"I know, and I'm sorry," Lucille Marcuse said. Tasha crept deeper into the barn, toward the sound of Lucille's voice. "But what's done is done. You have to leave. You have to get out of here now. There's no time to waste."

There was a door up ahead. It was old and decrepit like the rest of the barn, and hung half-open. Tasha tiptoed toward it, hardly daring to breathe as she moved. Finally she was in a position to peek inside a section of the barn that seemed to be made up of stables, all of them empty and musty-smelling. She saw Lucille Marcuse pleading with a man who stood with his back to Tasha.

"I have my car outside," Lucille was saying.

"Go and pack, and I'll drive you to the airport."

"And where do you suggest I go?" the man said. He was tall and slender and wore a hat that covered his head so completely that Tasha couldn't tell what colour his hair was. As bright and yellow as a buttercup, she suspected. She wished that the man would turn to the side a little so she could see if his face was tattooed.

"It doesn't matter where you go," Lucille said, "just as long as you get out of here right now. We don't have any time to spare."

Lucille Marcuse started toward the man and grabbed one of his hands. Tasha saw that it was a very old hand, weathered and wrinkled. She scuttled backward to keep herself hidden, and tripped. Suddenly she was flying backwards, her arms pinwheeling as she tried to find a handhold, something to help her stay upright. No such luck. She crashed to the ground, blinking her eyes shut on impact. When she opened them again she was staring up into the leathery face of Evart Horstbueller.

Chapter Fourteen

"Natasha." Her name was like a sigh when spoken by Evart Horstbueller.

Tasha stared up at the weather-beaten old face. It really was him. Her eyes weren't playing tricks on her. When she started to get up, he extended a hand to help her.

"I thought — "

"Never mind what you thought," Lucille Marcuse snapped. Her voice was as cold as the glint of the gun she held in her hand. Tasha's eyes widened at the sight of it. She'd never seen a real gun before, certainly not one pointed directly at her. Evart Horstbueller followed Tasha's gaze. He clucked in annoyance when he saw what she was looking at.

"For heaven's sake, Lucille, she's just a child. Put that thing away before you hurt someone."

But Lucille didn't lower the gun. "She may be a child," she said, "but that doesn't mean she isn't dangerous. If she didn't know before that you're still alive, she knows now. You have to leave, Father. You can't stay here any longer."

Tasha's mind raced as she tried to take in what was happening. Everyone had told her that Evart Horstbueller had died five years ago, shortly after her mother had disappeared. But he was standing right here in front of her. And his daughter, who was pointing a gun directly at Tasha, was telling him that he had to flee. It could all add up to only one thing.

"It was *you*!" Tasha said. "You killed my mother. You killed her and then faked your own death so you wouldn't get caught." There was just one thing she didn't understand. "But *why*?" she asked. "My mother liked you. She respected you. And I thought you liked her. Why did you do it?"

Evart Horstbueller looked at her with pale, sad eyes. "Natasha — "

"Go into the house, Father. Go into the house and pack. I'll take care of her."

"Take care of her?" Evart Horstbueller shook his head in disgust. "What do you intend to do? Shoot her?"

"I'll lock her in the tractor barn. That will give you time to get away."

"Then what?" he said. Tasha noticed again how weary he sounded. "You can't keep her locked up forever. You'll have to let her go eventually. When you do, she'll go straight to the police."

"Maybe," Lucille conceded. "But by then it won't matter. By then you'll be long gone."

"And what about you, Lucille? Once they know I'm still alive, your life will be in danger."

"Then I'll go with you. Please, Father! You

know what will happen if you stay."

Evart Horstbueller stood still for a long time, staring first at Tasha, then at the dusty floor of the old barn. Finally he heaved his bony shoulders in an elaborate shrug.

"I'm sorry, Natasha," he said. "I'm truly sorry." As he turned and walked past Tasha, Lucille gestured with her gun.

"That way," she said. "Very slowly. No sudden moves. I don't want to hurt you, but if I have to choose between you and my father, I think you know what I'll do."

Tasha knew only too well. As she walked slowly through the barn and out into the yard, allowing herself to be guided toward the sturdiest looking building on the property, a metal-framed garage that Lucille called a tractor barn, Tasha wondered where Jace was. Was he watching what was happening? Had he already gone for help? Surely he wouldn't risk trying to disarm Lucille. For a piano teacher, she seemed to have a pretty sure grip on the gun. She also seemed determined to protect her father from the police.

"Get inside there," Lucille ordered when they reached the tractor barn.

Tasha saw a huge padlock hanging from its door. The garage itself was dark inside. There were no windows that Tasha could see.

"I said, inside," Lucille growled, prodding her with the gun.

Then suddenly, as if she'd been scalded, Lucille let out a yowl. Tasha whirled around to see the gun fly from Lucille's hand. It glinted in the sunlight as it spun through the air. Lucille was doubled over, her left hand grasping her right wrist. Behind her stood Jace, his face twisted with pain.

"The gun!" he shouted at Tasha. "Get the gun!" Then, "Jeeze, this karate chop stuff is a lot more painful in real life than it looks in the movies. I think I broke something."

Tasha dove for the gun. Her hand was just about to close around it when Evart Horstbueller came out of the house, carrying what looked to Tasha like a rifle.

"Don't touch that gun!" screamed Lucille behind Tasha. "Father, don't let her get the gun."

Evart Horstbueller looked at Tasha reaching for the weapon. He looked at Lucille, her face contorted. Then he lowered his rifle and said, "No more."

For a few moments Tasha didn't move. She didn't trust what was happening. Evart Horstbueller was a murderer. He had killed her mother and buried her in the basement of the Fireside Café. He couldn't be giving up so quickly. Maybe he was waiting for her to grab the gun. Maybe . . .

Evart Horstbueller put his rifle down, came across the yard and bent to retrieve the gun. He emptied it of its bullets, then lobbed it into a thicket beside the tractor barn.

"Why don't you and your friend come inside, Natasha?" he said. "We'll have a cup of tea."

* * *

The farmhouse that from the outside had looked so dilapidated was, inside, immaculately clean and simply but brightly furnished. The kitchen floor tile gleamed in the sunlight that streamed through the window. The kitchen counters were clean and uncluttered. Even the burner plates on the big gas stove sparkled.

"Please," Evart Horstbueller said, "sit."

Nobody moved toward the pine chairs that circled the kitchen table. The last thing Tasha wanted from her mother's murderer was a cup of tea. She didn't trust him either. His hospitality was probably intended to disarm her. Lucille stared sulkily at her father as he put the kettle on to boil, clearly convinced that he was doing the wrong thing. Jace, edgy, kept peering out the window.

Evart Horstbueller lit the gas under the kettle. As he reached for the tea canister on the counter he looked at all three of them and shook his head. "I would never hurt your mother, Tasha," he said.

"Father, please —"

Evart Horstbueller silenced her with a wave of his hand. "For the past five years, I thought that staying out here was the best thing to do. After all, who was being hurt? The worst had already happened, but nobody even realized it. Everyone thought Catherine — your mother — had left Leonard. No one knew what had really happened, so it was easy to tell myself that by hiding out here — " he gazed around the sunny kitchen " — I was hurting no one and I was saving myself." His eyes brimmed with sadness as he looked at Lucille. "I even managed to convince myself that I was doing this for Lucille, so that she would be safe. But now— " he shook his head " — now I know I was being a coward. I should have come forward as soon as I heard that Leonard had been arrested." He shook his head again. "What I did was wrong, Tasha. I'm sorry."

Tasha was confused. The way he was talking, it sounded as if he were saying he hadn't committed murder after all. But if that were so, why was he hiding out here, and why had Lucille held Tasha at gunpoint to give him time to get away?

"I don't understand," she said. "You killed my mother, didn't you?"

"No," Evart Horstbueller said. "Although sometimes — whenever I think about it — I think that keeping silent all these years makes me no better than a murderer. But, no, I did not do it."

"Then why — "

"Why am I hiding here?"

Tasha nodded.

"Father, please don't — " Lucille began.

Evart Horstbueller shook his head wearily. "I have been hiding for seven years."

"*Seven* years?" Tasha said. "But it's only been five years since my mother . . . since she . . . "

"Father — "

"No, Lucille. The time for secrets is over. Now is the time for truth." He turned back to Tasha. "Let me try to explain. Seven years ago, back in Holland, my wife was killed in a hit-and-run accident. The man who was responsible was given a suspended sentence. A suspended sentence!" He spoke the words bitterly. "He deserved far worse, for what he did."

Tasha glanced at Jace, who looked as confused as she was.

"I don't understand," she said.

"Not long after this man was released, he was murdered." Evart paused a moment. "I was accused of the crime."

"I suppose you're going to tell us you didn't do it," Jace said.

"He didn't," Lucille blurted.

"I didn't," Evart Horstbueller said. "But so many people had heard me threaten him. It was stupid. I wasn't going to harm him. But when you lose someone you love, you do crazy things." His shoulders sagged. "Everyone remembered what I had threatened. So when I was charged, I did another stupid thing. I didn't trust the courts. How could I, when the man who killed my wife was let off so easily? So I — " He hesitated and frowned. "Skipped bail, is that how you say it?"

"That's how you say it," Jace said, shaking his head in disbelief.

"I skipped bail," Evart said, "left the country, came here with Lucille, and assumed a new identity."

Tasha stared at the old man in stunned silence. When she was little, he always had a piece of cake or a slice of pie set aside for her in the Café's kitchen, and never failed to let her lick the bowl from a batch of fudge frosting. She couldn't imagine him killing anyone. Finally she said, "But I don't understand what this has to do with my mother."

"Your mother knew," Evart said.

Tasha frowned. "Even if she did, I still don't see what all this has to do with her."

He shook his head. "Let me finish, Tasha. I

didn't kill your mother. But I know who did. That's why I've been hiding here, pretending to be dead. I know who did it, and all this time I've been afraid — afraid for my own life, even more afraid for Lucille."

Tasha glanced at Jace, who shrugged his confusion. "I don't understand," she said.

The kettle started to scream.

"Please," Evart Horstbueller said, "please, sit. I will explain everything."

"But Father, we don't have time for this — "

"Everything," he repeated. "Natasha has a right to know."

The tea in Tasha's mug grew cold as she listened to Evart Horstbueller's story.

"When I arrived in Canada, I changed my name and invented a new life for myself. I got a job in your parents' restaurant. Everything seemed fine. Then your mother took a trip to Europe."

"I remember that," Tasha said. Mostly what she remembered was her mother coming home again after a long absence, her eyes filled with the excitement of all she had seen, her arms filled with presents. "She brought me some wooden shoes."

Evart smiled gently. "While she was in Amsterdam, her purse was stolen."

"I remember that too," Tasha said. Another picture came to mind, this one of her father alternately soothing and firm as he spoke into the phone, calming Tasha's mother and helping her decide what to do. "Dad told her to go to the police station and report it."

"Which she did," Evart said. "While she was

there, she saw a poster with my face on it. For some reason — at the time I thought it was a miracle — Catherine said nothing to the police."

Tasha tried to imagine her mother making such a discovery — that someone she knew was wanted for murder — and keeping this information to herself as she reported her purse stolen. It didn't seem at all like a miracle to Tasha. It seemed exactly like something her mother would do.

"She always liked you," she said to Evart. "And she was always fair. She probably wanted to hear your side of the story before she said anything to anyone."

Evart nodded. His eyes grew misty. "After she returned, she asked me about it. And when I told her the truth, she said she believed me. Catherine was a wonderful woman. She even offered to lend me money to hire a detective to find the real killer." He raised a hand and wiped a tear from his eye. "I thought my secret was safe with your mother. But I found out that someone had overheard us talking."

"Who?" Tasha asked.

Evart didn't answer the question. He seemed to be off in another world, recalling old memories. Then he focussed on Tasha's face again. "She didn't want to be at the Café any more," he said. "She wanted to travel, and she wanted your father to sell the restaurant and go with her. Instead, he took on Denny Durant as a silent partner. Your mother was so angry when she found out. She didn't like Denny."

Tasha cocked her head. "Why not?"

"Because of the people he kept company with.

Denny's hockey career was over. Hardly anyone remembered him. But he still wanted to be a big shot. He did that by getting into the restaurant business and making friends with people who weren't very nice. He used to come to the Café every night and sit in a booth in the back — he called it his office — entertaining his friends. I don't think any of them really respected him, but they went along with him because with Denny there they had a place where they could hang out and transact their business."

"Business?" Jace said.

"Sometimes drug deals, sometimes getting rid of stolen goods, you name it."

"If things were so bad," Jace said, "why did you stay? Why didn't you quit?"

"He *was* going to leave," Lucille said. "He'd even given his notice to your father. He was due to leave the week after your mother . . . "

"One more week," Evart said. "It would have made all the difference in the world."

Tasha stared at Evart Horstbueller's weathered face, and drew in a deep breath. He had the answer. All she had to do was ask the question. Four simple words.

"What happened that night?"

Evart looked down at the table. He wrapped his hands around his mug as if it were a life preserver that could keep him from drowning in a sea of stormy memories.

"There was hardly anyone in the Café. Hardly any paying customers, that is. Just a few of Denny's *friends* — " He spoke the word with contempt.

" — eating and drinking for free. From where I was in the kitchen I could hear them arguing. Something about money. I couldn't stand it. All I wanted to do was close the Café and go home. Such a storm it was outside! Rico had already gone home, so I went to take out the garbage. When I came back in your mother was in the little room off the kitchen. You remember, the office."

Tasha nodded. As she listened now to Evart, she saw everything he described, as if she were listening to him read aloud to her while she sat with her eyes shut, imagining the scene, the actors, every movement:

There is her mother, standing in the small office, smiling sadly at Evart as she tells him she's come to say goodbye, that she's leaving Leonard. Then the shouting from the other room grows so loud that her mother has to raise her voice to make herself heard, until, finally, she becomes exasperated. "That Denny," she says, her voice sharp, "I don't know how Leonard puts up with him." She marches out through the kitchen and into the dining room to give Denny an earful. Evart scurries after her, tugging on her arm, telling her, "Catherine, no, leave him be, it's not worth it." But Catherine storms into the dining room just as one of Denny's friends says, "I didn't bump off those two armoured car guys for nothing . . . " When the meaning of these words sinks in, she stops so suddenly that Evart, chasing her, bumps into her.

"There had been a big robbery about a week before," Evart went on. "Two armoured car drivers were killed. Nearly a million dollars was stolen. It had been in the papers all week. And here were the two men who had done it, and they had just said so, right out loud. Even Denny looked shocked."

As did Catherine, and Evart. Tasha pictured the shock on their faces as they stared at the man who had spoken. A man with terrible black eyes who had just confessed to murder.

"For a few moments," Evart said, "the room was as still as death. Then Denny said, 'Catherine! What brings you out on a night like this?' He spoke as if he was delighted to see her. At first Catherine was confused. So was I. Why would Denny sound so happy? Hadn't we all just heard a confession to murder? Then I saw the desperation in his eyes. He seemed to be begging us to play along, to pretend we'd heard nothing out of the ordinary."

Tasha nodded, her hands gripping the edge of the clean-scrubbed table.

"Your mother was a quick thinker. I couldn't believe what she did next. She answered Denny as calmly as if she had just bumped into him on the street," Evart said. "She told him that Leonard was at home, that she'd left him and was on her way to the airport. 'Evart's seeing me off,' she said. 'I have a taxi waiting outside.' The whole time she was talking, she was slowly backing toward the door, with me just beside her. We were both trying to stay calm. I don't know about Catherine, but I thought maybe we might get away. I thought we had a chance."

Tasha caught her breath. Here was the moment she was waiting for, that she had been dreading. She could feel it coming. *I thought we had a chance.*

"But?" Tasha said. "What happened?"

"The two men with Denny stopped us. One of them blocked our way. The other pulled a knife. Catherine saw what was happening. She did the only thing she could do. She started to scream. That's when the man with the knife attacked her. He stabbed her again and again, even after she crumpled to the floor." Evart's voice was a monotone. "I saw it. I saw it, and I said nothing. I — I couldn't get a sound out."

Tasha put her hands to her eyes to block the horror. Her poor mother. She'd stumbled into the wrong place at the wrong time, and no one, no one had done anything to help her.

"Denny . . . " she gasped. "Denny Durant was there? He saw all of this?"

Evart nodded. "I wanted to run, but I was afraid that if I made a move they would kill me too. Denny also looked scared. He said, 'So, what are you going to do now? Are you going to kill us too?'"

"But how come they didn't?" Jace asked. When Lucille gave him a sharp look, he added, "No offence."

"One of them, not the one with the knife but the other one, said, 'We wouldn't kill you, Denny. We know you're an okay guy. You *are*, aren't you, Denny?' Denny nodded. Then the man said, 'You're going to prove what an okay guy you are. You're going to prove it by killing the German.' He meant me."

"They wanted Denny to *kill* you?" Tasha asked, appalled.

"If Denny killed me, they said, then none of

186

them would be able to go to the police. They'd all be guilty of murder."

"But Denny didn't."

Evart shook his head. "Denny may not be as tough as he thinks he is, but he's smart. He told them they weren't thinking straight. 'Killing the woman was one thing,' he said. 'As far as anyone knows, she left her husband, she left town. Grab her suitcase and send away that taxi and you're home free.' He said he could fix it so everyone thought she was safe and sound on the other side of the country. Nobody would even look for her."

The letters, Tasha realized. It was Denny who had written the letters from Vancouver. Denny knew Tasha's nickname.

"He told them that I was a different story," Evart went on. "He said that Lucille came to pick me up every night, and that if I went missing she'd call the police. I thought he was crazy, that he wasn't going to be able to talk those two out of another killing. Then he said, 'Old Evart understands the importance of keeping his mouth shut, don't you, Evart? He knows it'll be better for him — and for his daughter — if he just makes like nothing happened here tonight.' The killers thought he was crazy. 'You trust this guy to keep his mouth shut?' they asked. Denny told them trust had nothing to do with it."

Suddenly it all came clear to Tasha. "It was *Denny* who overheard you and my mother talking about your past."

"And he used it against my father," Lucille said. "Denny told him that if he said a word about what

187

had happened, he would call the police and have Father arrested and sent back to the Netherlands. He said he'd make sure my whereabouts were known."

"Denny should have been a salesman," Evart said, "because he actually did it. He talked them out of making him kill me. And then — " He stifled an anguished sob.

"Oh Father — "

"No," Evart said. "No, I must tell it. These friends — " he spat the word " — these friends of Denny's made Denny and me help dig the hole in the basement. They took pictures of us digging and said they'd use them against us if they had to. They'd say we were in on it. They'd say we were as responsible for your mother's death as they were. And they told Denny if it ever came to light, both of us would die."

Tasha wanted to cover her ears. She wanted to shut out the horrible truth she was hearing, but she knew she couldn't, not if she was going to save her father, not if she was going to bring her mother's real killers to justice.

"I can see why you didn't go to the police," Jace said. "But then, why fake your death? And how?"

Evart stared down at the table. He looked older than when he had started his tale, and smaller. His shoulders slumped. "I didn't trust Denny or his friends," he said. "I didn't want to take the chance that they would tell the police back home where I was. I had to protect Lucille."

"We thought the only way we could be safe was if my father were thought to be dead," Lucille said. "So we arranged an accident. A fiery car crash."

"But how could you?" Jace shook his head. "There had to have been a body."

Tasha remembered what Enrico Zapata had told them. "Lucille's husband works at a funeral home," she said.

For the first time during the whole unravelling of the story Lucille refused to meet her gaze. "Herbert and I had only been dating for a few months. But when I told him I needed help, he knew exactly what to do. At the funeral home where he worked, he sometimes had to arrange burials of indigents for the city," she said. "He had been contracted to bury a man who died in a fire in an abandoned warehouse."

"So he buried that man as your father?"

Lucille nodded.

"I've been hiding out here ever since," Evart said. "Now it's time for the hiding to end." He offered Tasha a wan smile. "I'm so very sorry," he said. "It was wrong of me not to have come forward earlier. I couldn't save your mother, but I *can* help your father."

"And you can see to it that Denny and his friends get what they deserve," Tasha said quietly.

No one spoke for a moment. Then Lucille said, "I'll drive you into town, Father."

Tasha exchanged glances with Jace. She wasn't sure whether Lucille was in complete agreement with her father's decision to come out of hiding.

"If it's okay with everyone, I think we should take my car," Jace said. "It's just up the road."

Lucille bridled. "Are you saying you don't trust me?"

189

"Lucille," her father said gently. "Do you blame him? It's all right. We'll use your car, young man."

They waited while he cleaned up the tea things and changed his clothes. Then, when Jace opened the door to let him pass, a shot rang out, and Evart Horstbueller crumpled to the floor.

Chapter Fifteen

Tasha, Jace and Lucille scrambled back inside the farmhouse, pulling Evart with them. He was conscious, but his right arm hung limp at his side. Blood dripped from his hand onto the immaculate tile of the kitchen floor. Frantic and sobbing, Lucille directed them into the living room. Tasha and Jace helped Evart to the couch while Lucille ran upstairs for a first-aid kit. She also carried a snow-white pillowcase, which she tore into strips. Her hands trembled as she hurried to bandage her father's arm. Jace closed all the blinds and curtains so that whoever was outside couldn't see in.

"Where's the phone?" Tasha asked.

"There *is* no phone, remember?" Jace said.

Tasha looked at Evart for confirmation, and was bitterly disappointed when she got it.

"I thought the less dealings I had with anyone in the outside world, including the phone company, the less chance there was that anyone would find out

I was still alive," he said. "Lucille — " He winced. "Lucille wouldn't even let me use a cell phone out here. She thought there was a risk of being traced."

Tasha glanced at Lucille.

"Cell phones aren't secure," Lucille said. "They're too easy to eavesdrop on. Anyone could have overheard me talking to father. And Denny knew where I lived, even after I married. I figured he'd be keeping an eye on me, just in case."

Jace crept close to the door and tried to peer out. Tasha ran to him and pulled him aside.

"Whoever's out there might see you," she cried. Her heart hammered in her chest. Someone out there had shot at them. Whoever it was had wounded Evart. He — or she — could just as easily have hit her, or Jace.

"If there's no phone to call for help, then we have to figure out a way to get out of here," Jace said.

"There's a portable phone in my car," Lucille said. "In the glove compartment." She was binding strips of pillowcase securely around her father's wound.

A lot of good that was, Tasha thought. Lucille's car was parked in the middle of the yard, about thirty metres from the front door. The gunman was out there.

"What about your gun?" Tasha asked. "Where is it?"

"Still outside," Lucille muttered. "The bullets are out there, too. Someone — " she looked pointedly at her father, whose face was as white as his bandage " — emptied them out into the yard, remember?"

"The rifle, then," Tasha said. Evart had brought it back into the house.

"It's a shotgun," Evart said, "not a rifle. And it hasn't been fired for years. I found it in the barn after we bought this place. I don't even have any ammunition for it."

Tasha's mind was racing. No ammunition for the gun was just about the last straw, even though she wouldn't have known what to do with a loaded shotgun if she had one.

Lucille looked even unhappier than Tasha. "Father, I thought we agreed — "

"What did we agree?" Evart Horstbueller said. "That I would spend the rest of my days living like a man in a wild west movie? That I would live confined to my own land with a loaded gun always in my hand? No, Lucille, I don't want that. I never wanted that."

"But, Father — "

"Excuse me, I hate to interrupt," Jace cut in. "But something — *someone* — just moved out there. We have to do something, fast, before whoever it is figures out that there's not much we *can* do and comes in here and . . . well, you know."

"I don't suppose you have a suggestion?" Lucille said.

"We have to get to your car," Tasha said. "We have to get that phone and call the police."

"But how?" Jace asked. He was drumming his fingers on the tabletop. "Maybe we could create some kind of diversion, distract whoever's out there so that I can go out the back and circle around to the car." He shook his head. "That's nuts, right? The guy has a gun. If we create a diversion, he might just start shooting. This time he could *kill* someone."

Tasha thought for a minute. She didn't know how much the man out there had seen. Did he know that Evart had thrown Lucille's gun across the yard? Did he know that they had a useless shotgun in the house with them? Suppose he didn't.

"Maybe we should just do nothing," she said.

"What?" Lucille snorted. "Do you think if we do nothing he'll just go away?"

"He'll either wait — "

"I don't think he'll wait too long," Jace said. His voice had gone a pitch higher. "I just saw something move out there again."

"Suppose he came here to kill us all, or at least to kill Mr. Horstbueller," Tasha said. "And suppose he thinks we're helpless, completely unarmed."

"Which we *are*," Lucille said. She looked acidly at her father, still blaming him, Tasha guessed, for chucking her gun into the weeds.

"If we don't go out there, he's going to have to come in. If he thinks we're unarmed, he probably also thinks there's nothing much that could happen to him if he does come in."

"He'd be right," Lucille said. "If he comes in here with a gun, it will be like shooting fish in a barrel. And we'll be the fish."

"Get the shotgun, Jace," Tasha said.

"But it's not loaded," Lucille wailed.

Evart's eyes twinkled. "But *he* doesn't know that, right, Natasha?"

"But — "

"Get the shotgun, Lucille," Evart repeated. His

tone made it clear that he would accept no argument.

"We'd better get something to tie him up, too," Tasha said. "Do you have any rope, Mr. Horstbueller?"

"In the cellar," he said. Jace ran to fetch it.

Something creaked on the porch just as Lucille came back with the shotgun. When she heard it, she let out a small mewling sound.

"He's there," Jace whispered.

Tasha's knees buckled. There was a man with a gun out on Evart's porch, a man who had already used it once. He was getting closer and obviously meant to do more harm.

"Go to the back door and wait there," Tasha told Jace. "When he comes in, run to Lucille's car, get the phone, then run for cover and call the police." There was a chance, a good chance, that he could make it, so long as whoever was out there stayed in the house long enough, and so long as Jace was fast.

"What about you?"

Tasha took the shotgun from Lucille. "I'm going to be behind the front door, with this. Lucille, you sit beside your father on the couch. Just sit quietly."

Jace grabbed at the shotgun. "*I'll* stay here," he said. "*You* run for the phone."

Tasha knew what he was trying to do. He thought it would be safer out there once the gunman was in the house. He wanted to protect her. She shook her head. "*I'm* doing this, Jace, and there's no way you can talk me out of it — " She broke off as the front doorknob turned ever so slightly.

Lucille gasped and sank down onto the sofa next to her father.

Tasha nodded toward the back door, and Jace, in a crouch, headed for it. He glanced back at her, worried, but he didn't argue. Instead he stationed himself beside the door, ready to sprint around the house to Lucille's car.

Tasha backed herself against the wall behind the front door. Half of her wished the man out there would go away and leave them alone. But she knew that wasn't going to happen. So the rest of her wished that he'd hurry up, that he'd shove open the door, burst right in, and they could just do it.

The house was completely silent. Lucille sat rigid beside her father, who looked desperately pale. The bandage on his arm was soaked with blood. He needed medical treatment as soon as possible, Tasha realized. If he didn't get it, he stood a good chance of bleeding to death.

She held her breath and waited. Time and reality lost all meaning. Never could she have dreamed she'd be in this position, pressed up against a wall behind a door, an empty shotgun in her hand, waiting for an armed man to burst into the house and start shooting at her. She felt like someone on a TV show, except that TV heroes were never truly scared for their lives. She was.

Her eyes were focussed on the doorknob. She'd have her cue when it started to turn.

Nothing happened.

Then all of a sudden the doorknob spun around and the front door flew open. Tasha saw Lucille sit bolt upright on the couch, her eyes wide open in terror, her hand stuffed into her mouth so she wouldn't scream. Run, Jace, Tasha thought. Run!

"Well, well," a voice said, "how convenient." The man who spoke was tall and muscular. His hair was exactly as Mrs. Zadoor had described it — brilliant yellow, as bright as a buttercup. "Now, where are your little friends?"

Just like on TV, Tasha thought. Then she thought, this is crazy. I'm about to step out from behind this door and point a completely useless shotgun at the back of a man who is obviously a killer, and I'm *still* thinking this can't be happening to me. But it *is* happening. She crept out from behind the door, pressed the barrel of the shotgun into the man's back, and said, in a voice pitched so deep that even to her it sounded almost masculine, "Drop your gun."

On TV the man would have dropped it. On TV the two people on the couch would have jumped up and tied the hands of the man who'd just dropped the gun. Then there would be a commercial, and the next thing you knew, the police would be there and justice would have been done.

But this man didn't drop his gun. As far as Tasha could tell, he didn't even lower it. He said, in a very cool voice, "What have we here? What are you planning to do, kid — "

How did he know she was just a kid? Tasha wondered. He must have seen them. He'd seen two adults and two kids, and there were the adults right in front of him. It was obvious from his voice and from the way he just stood there, hanging onto his gun, that he wasn't worried. "What are you planning to do, kid? Shoot me in the back?" As if he knew that she wouldn't, even if her gun was loaded.

Which it wasn't. And which, for all she knew, *he* knew too.

"I didn't think so," the man said, his voice mocking, as if he were speaking to a very small child.

As he started to turn Tasha saw a jagged scar on his cheek. Mrs. Zadoor had been right. It did look like a bird, although Tasha could never have guessed what kind of bird. But one thing was sure: this was the man who had pushed Mrs. Mercer down the stairs. This was the man who had shot at Evart Horstbueller. If she didn't do something, try something, anything, no matter how feeble the attempt, he would do far worse.

She upended the shotgun so she could grasp the barrel in her hand, and as the man turned, she swung, as hard as she could. The shotgun grip bounced off the man's head and sent him reeling in one direction. His hair shot off in another. It took Tasha a moment to realize that the bright yellow hair was a wig.

The man swore. Tasha grimaced. That was bad. If he was able to swear, she hadn't succeeded in knocking him out. Nothing turned out in real life the way it did on TV. But as he fell his gun flew out of his hand and arced through the air. Both man and gun hit the ground at approximately the same time, but a couple of metres apart. Tasha dove for the weapon. Lucille propelled herself into action and dove for a large ceramic pot.

The man groaned after he landed, then shook his head as if to clear it. His eyes seemed to focus at the precise moment that Tasha's hand closed on his gun. He let out a roar and threw himself forward on all fours trying to get to his feet.

Staggering a little he turned toward Tasha, who held the gun in trembling hands. This gun was loaded. It could do real damage. Suppose she pulled the trigger. Suppose the gun went off. But suppose it didn't hit the man who was advancing on her, but hit someone else instead? Lucille, or Evart?

Seeing her hesitation, the man gave her a slow, malevolent sneer. He stretched out a hand.

"That's right, kid," he said. "Hand over the gun. Hand it over before you hurt yourself."

Then suddenly he crumpled to the floor amid shards of pottery. Lucille stood behind him, looking stunned by her success. She had toppled the giant.

Tasha stared down at the gun in her hand, then over at Evart. He stretched out his hand, and she gratefully surrendered the gun to him.

"We'd better tie him up," she said to Lucille, "before he wakes up."

They both froze when they heard something creak out on the porch. Oh no! Tasha thought. What if Birdface hadn't come out here alone? What if he had someone with him? What if that someone had dealt with Jace and was now out on the porch, preparing to burst in on them, guns blazing? What if —

"Jace?" Tasha called cautiously. "Jace, is that you?"

"Tash? Tasha, are you okay?"

Tasha didn't open the door, not yet. The accomplice, if the man on the floor now being trussed by Lucille had an accomplice, could have caught Jace and been holding him, a gun pointed at his head, even as he forced Jace to answer.

"Are *you* okay, Jace?" Tasha called.

"Yeah. Is it safe to come in?"

Tasha glanced at Evart, who must have had the same idea, because his entire attention was turned to the front door, and he held the gun firmly in his grip.

"Yeah, it's safe," Tasha called. "Come on."

She held her breath as the door opened. Jace was alone. He held a portable phone in his hand.

"I called the cops. They're on their way," he said. He stared at the man lying on the floor, then at Lucille as she worked at tying him up. "Remember when you thought we were being followed, Tash? There's a black T-bird parked up the road. I think it belongs to this guy."

"He's the one," Evart said. His voice was hoarse. "Natasha, he's the one who killed your mother."

Tasha stared down at the man with the bird-shaped scar on his cheek. He was a big man with a crooked nose that looked like it had been broken at least once, and with big hands with knobbly knuckles. Killer hands, she thought. This was him . . . This was the man . . .

"Tash?" Jace's voice seemed to be coming at her from a million miles away. The whole room seemed to be swirling around her. "Hey, Tash, you look awfully pale — "

She couldn't hold it in any longer. She bolted from the house, ran across the yard to a weed patch, and threw up everything she had eaten that day. Then she burst into tears.

Chapter Sixteen

Whenever Tasha thought about it — and she had thought about it often, she had even dreamed about it — she thought it would happen like this: She would find the magical piece of evidence she needed, the one incontrovertible fact that would force the police to see that her father couldn't possibly have done what he was accused of. They would release him immediately. The emphasis, in her thoughts, was always on the *immediate* part of it. Her father was innocent, therefore he would be free to go.

In fact, his release was anything but immediate. Detectives Marchand and Pirelli asked Tasha a million questions. Then they wanted to talk to Evart Horstbueller alone. That took forever. Tasha later learned that they'd made him repeat his story several times. Finally, on the basis of what he told them, they added a charge of murder to the attempted murder charge they'd already laid against Birdface. They also sent someone to bring in Denny Durant.

Only then, hours after Tasha and Jace, Lucille Marcuse and Evart Horstbueller had arrived at the police station with Birdface, did they drop all charges against Leonard Scanlan.

"What about the third man?" Tasha asked. "There were two men in the Café with Denny that night."

"We have Mr. Horstbueller's description of him," Detective Marchand said. "And I have a feeling we'll be able to get Denny to cooperate with us."

Tasha nodded. "I want to see my father," she said.

"We'll give you a lift to the hospital," Detective Marchand said.

"It's okay," Jace said, "I'll take her."

Detective Marchand shrugged. "It's up to you, of course, Tasha. But I'd like to go with you. I arrested your father, I'd like to be there when he finds out he's a free man."

If she lived to be a hundred, and forgot everything else about her life — her childhood, the address of the house she had first lived in, her own name — Tasha knew she would never forget the moment her father learned that he was no longer under arrest. His eyes, initially dull, grew bright, like a fire being fanned, and he struggled to sit up in his bed. He stared at Detective Marchand for a few moments, then opened his mouth and said exactly two words: "Thank you."

"It's your daughter you have to thank," the detective said. "She refused to believe you were guilty. And she was right. She proved it."

Leonard Scanlan turned to Tasha and stretched

out his arms. She ran to him and felt a new strength as he hugged her.

* * *

"Dad?"

Leonard Scanlan looked up from the sauce he was stirring. On the other side of the kitchen, Aunt Cynthia was cutting up vegetables for a salad.

"There's something I don't understand, Dad." Tasha had been hesitating about asking. What if he didn't want to answer her question? What if she only stirred up more painful memories and made him sad again? She couldn't bear the thought of saying anything that would hurt him, after what he'd tried to do to himself at the jail.

"Like what?" he asked.

Should she ask? She wanted to know — *how* she wanted to know — but would the asking be worse than the answer? Would she end up sorry that she had spoken?

"When you went out that night, you said you went for a drive, but *where* did you go?" Tasha asked. "Were you trying to find Mom and bring her back?"

This time when he looked down, Leonard Scanlan didn't look up again for a very long time.

"I was trying to figure out how I was going to manage without her," he said at last. "Your mother and I had grown so far apart. I thought— I thought maybe she'd found someone else and that's why she was leaving. I didn't know how I was going to be able to carry on without her." His voice cracked. He paused for a moment, and Tasha saw that he was struggling to control himself. "I'm sorry I left you alone, but I had to think. Finally I decided to come home and wait to see what your mother was going to do next. And then I got those letters — "

"Denny wrote them."

"I know that now," her father said. His eyes glistened with unshed tears. "All these years," he said, "I've been business partners with someone who knew what happened, someone who was in on it and never said anything to me. The murderer was an old teammate of his! All these years . . . "

"There's no way you could have known, Dad."

"If only I'd done what your mother wanted. If only I'd put her wishes first for a change. She wouldn't have gone to the Café that night. She wouldn't have stumbled into that whole terrible situation. She wouldn't — "

If only. The two sorriest words in the English language. Tasha got up and went to her father. "You couldn't have known, Dad. Nobody knew."

Her father shook his head, as if not wanting to accept what she said. Finally, reluctantly, he said, "I know. And I know that even if I'd listened to her, there'd be no guarantee she would have stayed. We'd grown so far apart. She still might have left, but maybe not that night. Everything would have been different for you, Tasha. You wouldn't have spent the past five years wondering what happened, wondering why she never contacted you."

Tasha blinked hard to keep tears from her eyes. "It's okay, Dad," she whispered. "It's okay."

They clung to each other for a long time.

* * *

More than five years after her death, Catherine Scanlan was given a proper burial. Tasha had expected to feel overwhelming sorrow at the funeral. Instead she felt a sense of completion, along with relief that it was all over.

As she and Leonard Scanlan left the cemetery, Detectives Marchand and Pirelli approached them.

"Edith Mercer regained consciousness yesterday," Detective Marchand said. "We thought you'd like to know."

"Is she okay?" Tasha asked.

"It looks hopeful. The doctors think she might make an almost complete recovery if she's lucky." She smiled softly at Tasha. "She confirmed Mrs. Zadoor's story. She *was* pushed down the stairs, and it was by a man with a bird on his face — a bird-shaped scar."

"The same man who killed my mother," Tasha said.

Detective Marchand nodded. "It seems Mrs. Mercer was sitting in front of her big window that night. She saw your mother arrive by taxi at the Café. Then, a few minutes later, she saw a man come out and pay the taxi driver. That man, Birdface, looked up and saw her watching. The next day he came up to her on the street and said, 'Some people are too nosy for their own good; curiosity killed the cat.' At the time Mrs. Mercer thought that whatever he was talking about had something to do with the disreputable crowd that hung around the Café. She didn't think about it again until after your mother was found and she saw the same man outside her apartment, watching her."

"Birdface, you mean?"

Detective Marchand nodded. "She saw him

twice. It scared her, because now she was beginning to understand what she'd seen five years ago."

"If she was scared," Tasha said, "why did she invite Jace and me up to her apartment?"

"I think you took her by surprise. And she probably felt sorry for you, knowing what she did. But she wasn't prepared for your questions. You really threw her when you started asking her what she'd seen that night. And when Denny had you followed and found out that you'd talked to Mrs. Mercer — "

"He tried to get her out of the way."

Detective Marchand nodded. "He sent Birdface to silence her."

Tasha nodded. There was one thing she still didn't understand.

"Why did he wear that wig, though, and such a brightly coloured one?"

"Maybe to draw attention away from his scar," Detective Marchand said. "So that we'd be looking for someone with bright yellow hair. And, Tasha? I was right about Denny. He was only too willing to cooperate. He told us who the third man was. We picked him up this morning."

Tasha nodded. Her mother was finally laid to rest. Now all that needed to happen was that Denny Durant and his friends be brought to justice.

"What's going to happen to Evart Horstbueller?" she asked.

Detective Marchand shrugged. "He has to go back to Holland to sort things out. The murder charge against him has been dropped. Apparently it was dropped four years ago. It seems the real murderer admitted to someone else that he'd done it, and that person reported it to the police."

"You mean Evart was hiding for *nothing* all these years?"

"Apparently," the detective said. "He still has to answer to charges relating to his flight from Holland. And, of course, there's his illegal immigration to Canada, plus that faked death to sort out. But I think he's going to be okay. His daughter is well established here, and a good person, it seems, apart from taking part in that fake burial. I think he'll be able to return." She looked frankly at Tasha. "All's well that ends well, I guess."

Tasha nodded. "Thanks for coming," she said to both detectives. "Thanks for telling us."

* * *

"Well?" Tasha said. She held her arms out wide and spun around in her new blue dress. "What do you think?"

Aunt Cynthia looked up from the blouse she was ironing and whistled softly. "You look terrific!" she said.

"Too terrific, if you ask me," Leonard Scanlan said. "Exactly where are you going?"

"Out," Tasha said. "On a date."

Her father arched an eyebrow. "Date? With who?"

Tasha laughed. "Who do you think, Dad? With Jace." Finally, she thought to herself. They weren't just going to a movie together like two old friends. They were going on a real date, like two people who were more to each other than just friends.

"Have a terrific time," Aunt Cynthia said. "And

make sure you're up early tomorrow morning. I'm trying to get an early afternoon flight home, but I'd like to make us all a special brunch before I go. You could ask Jason to come — "

"Tomorrow?" Tasha looked at her father. "But I thought — "

Her father grinned. He slipped an arm around his sister-in-law's shoulders. "There's something I've been meaning to ask you, Cynthia," he said. "You see, I find myself with three restaurants and no partner. I was wondering — "

The doorbell rang and Tasha rushed to answer it. She was confident her father and her aunt would work something out. In the meantime, she intended to have the best evening of her life.

Norah McClintock

The Body in the Basement is Norah McClintock's fifth novel for young adults. Asked why most of her books have been for that age group, Norah says it's probably because ,"When I think of a story, I always think of someone who is about fifteen or sixteen. I don't know why. Maybe it's the fifteen-year-old inside me." Her memories of her teenage years have remained vivid — the boy problem, homework, exam jitters . . .

Although Norah has a full-time job as an editor, she still manages to write a novel a year. "I love to write because I love to read. . . . When I was young, I was fortunate to live two blocks from the public library . . . . At that time it cost ten cents to get a library card — I've never encountered a better bargain than that."

Norah's novels often deal with unusual relationships (a tall girl liking a short boy in *Shakespeare and Legs*, three half-sisters with three different fathers in *The Stepfather Game*) or mysteries (*Jack's Back*). Her most recent mystery, *Mistaken Identity*, won the Arthur Ellis Award for Crime Fiction.

Norah lives with her family in Toronto.